GET UP AND GHOST

A CHANTILLY ADAIR PARANORMAL COZY MYSTERY

CAROLYN RIDDER ASPENSON

Severn River
PUBLISHING

GET UP AND GHOST

Severn River Publishing
www.SevernRiverPublishing.com

ISBN: 978-1-951249-93-9 (Paperback)

The Lily Sprayberry Realtor Cozy Mystery Series

Deal Gone Dead

Decluttered and Dead

Signed, Sealed and Dead

Bidding War Break-In

Open House Heist

Realtor Rub Out

Foreclosure Fatality

Lily Sprayberry Novellas

The Scarecrow Snuff Out

The Claus Killing

Santa's Little Thief

The Chantilly Adair Paranormal Cozy Mystery Series

Get Up and Ghost

Ghosts Are People Too

Praying For Peace

Ghost From the Grave

Haunting Hooligans: A Chantilly Adair Novella

The Pooch Party Cozy Mystery Series

Pooches, Pumpkins, and Poison

Hounds, Harvest, and Homicide

Dogs, Dinners, and Death

The Holiday Hills Witch Cozy Mystery Series

There's a New Witch in Town

Witch This Way

The Angela Panther Mystery Series

Unfinished Business

Unbreakable Bonds

Uncharted Territory

Unexpected Outcomes

Unbinding Love

The Christmas Elf

The Ghosts

Undetermined Events

The Event

The Favor

Other Books

Mourning Crisis (The Funeral Fakers Series)

Join Carolyn's Newsletter List at

CarolynRidderAspenson.com

You'll receive a free novella as a thank you!

To My Kids
(who never read my books and won't ever see this!)

CHAPTER 1

Agnes Hamilton hanged herself from a ceiling rafter of the two story foyer of her home wearing her hand beaded wedding dress for a wedding that never happened. Lying on the ground below her was a letter from her fiancé, Josiah Dilts, saying he'd run off with another woman and planned to marry her.

Agnes was a tomboy of sorts and could lasso a bull better than half the men in town, so not a soul dared question how a twenty-year-old woman no more than five feet tall could get a rope all the way up to a rafter like that. Her pa, John Hamilton's ladder leaned up against the wall, and everyone in the town knew she used that, and even though she killed herself, and it was tragic, there was awe in the talk of her lassoing and roping skills ever since that fateful day in 1872.

Her pa was the one that found her. He'd come in from a two day trip to South Carolina to her hanging there, all bloated and swollen like. John Hamilton climbed up the ladder, reached for his little girl, and cut the rope. Rumor has it when she hit the ground, her arm came off.

"Oh gosh, whoever wrote this didn't understand the value of word choice." I sighed after reading the file for Hamilton House, a historic Georgia plantation home turned restaurant in my home town of Castleberry Georgia. "I can't believe that's what's written for a historic home like this."

Delphina Beauregard, or Del for short, the owner of Community Café, the best coffee shop this side of the Mason-Dixon Line, poured me a fresh cup of her most robust brew, Del's Geterdone. "You talkin' to yourself again, sugar pie?" Del came in a compact package with a head full of bleached blonde hair usually slicked back into a tight ponytail and a wrinkle free face any woman over forty-five would kill for, and she was upwards of sixty-something. With a warrior personality and a sword like tongue to match, people knew not to mess with her. Most people, anyway. Some hadn't figured it out yet, but they would eventually, whether they wanted to or not.

I stabbed my index finger onto the piece of paper. "Look at this. Who writes this stuff, kids in elementary school?"

She gazed at the document and read it out loud. When she finished, she walked away saying, "You're the gal with the big college diploma, you tell me."

I threw a packet of sugar at her backside as she sashayed away. "You're no help."

She flipped around and winked at me. "I filled your cup mighty fine, didn't I, sugar?"

"Yes, ma'am, you sure did." I breathed in the alluring, smoky scented coffee before taking another sip. I loved the aroma of freshly brewed steaming hot coffee, sometimes even more than the taste of the stuff itself. The fragrance wrapped around me like a warm, cozy blanket on a cold winter's night, and was a refreshing reminder of the eventual coming of fall during the never ending boiling summers of northern Georgia. And that's what we were in, a never ending bout of humid heat with temperatures topping out at ninety-eight degrees and higher every day for the past three weeks. August in Georgia was hotter than Hades. It was already the start of September, and the temperatures hadn't even begun to cool.

Thelma Sayers scooted her chair across the floor to my table. "What's that you're working on now, Chantilly?"

Del hollered at her from behind the counter. "There you go again scratching up my floor. Why can't you just sit in the chairs that go with the table?"

Thelma Sayers, Del's best friend, recently purchased a new pair of hearing aids, one of those fancy kind that probably cost more than they were worth. She adjusted the one in her right ear, the ear closest to the counter. "That's better. I don't want to hear that old bag yelling at me."

"In her defense, you're scratching her wood floor moving the chairs on it."

She rolled her heavily made up eyes. "Well, that's her problem. She knows I got me a bad sciatica, and I can't sit in those chairs without the cushions. If she got chairs to match this one, I wouldn't have to ruin her floor."

There wasn't much I could say to that. "I'm working on the new copy for the Hamilton House." I tucked my pencil behind my ear. "Do you know who wrote this originally?"

She moved her large leopard print glasses, ones that went out of style in the 80s and magnified her bright blue eyeshadow and dark black eyeliner, to the tip of her nose and held the paper down her stretched out arm. "'Course I do. That's Bubba Aldridge's work. You remember him, don't you?"

I grew up in Castleberry, Georgia, a cozy little town of two thousand about seventy-five miles north of Atlanta, but I went to college in Alabama—Go Auburn—and hadn't moved back until my divorce was finalized three months ago. Twenty-seven years away was a long time, even though I'd visit my parents quite often, especially during their illnesses, but Castleberry hadn't changed a bit.

My parents, Hank and Addie Hansard, died within months of each other while my ex-husband and I battled out the fine print of our failed marriage.

Thelma waved her hand in front of my face. "Honey, you in there?"

I'd been in stare mode, lost in the memories of a happier, simpler time. "Oh, I'm sorry. No, I can't say that I met him personally, but I certainly know of him from the historical society."

Thelma slurped her coffee and stared out the large café window. "Good ol' Bubba, God rest his soul. He was a good man, and he did a lot of good things for Castleberry, that's for sure. Never made it past the sixth grade though, what with having to take over being the man in his family and running the farm and all."

Way to make me feel bad there, Thelma. "I'll just tweak it a bit, and it'll be perfect." I opened my laptop and created a new document titled Hamilton House and typed away.

"Look at those fingers go." Thelma mimicked my typing by tapping her fingers on the round Formica table top. "If I could type like you, I'd have three columns a week instead of one."

"I think one of your gossip columns is just perfect."

Del hollered from behind the counter. "What she means is there ain't a soul in town that could handle reading more than one of those things you write."

Thelma twisted something on her hearing aid. "Did you hear that screeching? It was hurting my little ear."

I chuckled. "Those hearing aids work mighty fine, don't they?"

She pulled the one out of her right ear and set it on the table. "That ought to do the trick."

I giggled again and went back to my writing as she chatted away at me about the upcoming BBQ competition. "It's going to be so much fun. I love a good barbecue."

When I finished the rewrite, I asked her to read it, and she offered up rave reviews. "I think you told the story well, but what about the lassoing part? You don't mention that."

"I'm not sure that's something people need to know." I'd eliminated the mention of Agnes Hamilton taking her own life, instead only saying her father found her hanging from the rafter. Alluding to a tragic death felt more respectful to me, and I didn't want poor Agnes Hamilton's memory continually stained with an action that likely happened because of a clouded, broken mind.

Thelma's uniqueness aside, she had a kind heart. "Oh yes, I see. Nobody wants to be remembered for their mistakes."

Especially their last ones.

Thelma adjusted her Dolly Parton esque wig. So far I'd counted seven different styles; one I realized, for each day of the week. Today's choice, an ash white up 'do with a red and white polka dot scarf wrapped around the bun, matched perfectly with her white and red polka dot dress and red slip on sneakers. The sneakers, she'd once said, helped ease the pain of her bunions.

Del scooted out from behind the counter, complaining about the noise in the place the entire five steps to our table. "What's all the fuss about? You find a new place to sit all day yet, Thelma? Maybe something on the other side of Atlanta? Lord knows this place could use the quiet."

Thelma pushed herself up from the chair, groaning in the process, gripped the back and guided it slowly back to the other table. The metal chair legs screeching and whining as she did.

A dark shadow floated in front of us, and I glanced out the window to see if someone was coming inside, but saw nothing. When I turned back around, the shadow was gone.

Del shook her head. "Can't get rid of her no matter how hard I try. Even raised the price of her drink to three dollars, but she still comes around."

"And I don't pay it neither. Who pays three dollars for a cup of coffee?"

I wondered if the three men that founded Starbucks ever asked themselves that question. "Well ladies, I hate to miss any more of this endless but highly entertaining bickering thing you two love to do, but I have to get over to the office."

Del grunted and mumbled while Thelma waved and hollered, "You take care now, Chantilly. We'll see you tomorrow."

Those two women loved to hate each other, but they didn't fool anyone. All of Castleberry knew they were the best of friends no matter how poorly they treated each other. My mother used to laugh at their antics, and I remembered the day two years ago when Thelma's husband Charlie passed, how Mom said Delphina closed the café for a week and handled everything for Charlie's arrangements.

Frenemies didn't do that kind of thing, true friends and family did, and Del and Thelma were family, no matter how much Del liked to complain.

I walked the two blocks to the historical society on the corner of Main and Castleberry streets. The blazing hot sun beat down on my bare, pasty white arms, and I wished I'd thought to apply sunscreen before leaving home that morning. My half Irish skin and curly red hair stood the test of time, and no matter how much Vitamin D I soaked up, my freckled body just wouldn't tan.

Thanks, Mom, I thought. Though, to my benefit, at forty-five years old, the only wrinkles I could find on my body required me to perform circus acts in front of the mirror to see. Nobody was that flexible. I thanked my mom for that, too.

I enjoyed the walk even though the morning temperature had already hit eighty-six, and it wasn't even nine o'clock. The history of the buildings filling the street in the short distance was one of the reasons why I loved Castleberry, and the reason I'd chosen to take the job with the historical society. Each building shared their own hint into the past, to the lives lived before mine. The Castleberry Bank for example, was once the Volk Family home. The Volks came to Georgia from Germany in the early 1900's hoping to make a living raising chickens. Their success in chicken farming allowed them to build a large family home in town, where the patriarch, Daniel Volk, promised his wife Clara they'd live out their lives. The story said she'd always wanted a big home in the center of town, one that everyone could walk to for parties and celebrations. Daniel gave her that wish, and after they both passed, their children sold the property to the bank. They only sold under the premise that certain rooms on the main floor and all of the lower level would remain as a museum to honor the family, and the bank kept their side of the agreement.

I particularly admired the walk up front porch with the extra wide brick steps and the white rounded columns. The Volk home was the perfect example of Georgia history. A Plantation style, only smaller, and in the main part of town.

Castleberry's Main Street was what every romantic at heart wanted a small town to be. Crepe myrtle trees lined each sidewalk, providing shade for walkers and the occasional high school cross country practice run. Sometimes, when a fresh, calm breeze whipped through, the petals from the trees settled into my hair and I carried the fresh flowery scent with me the rest of the day.

Unlike other towns, Castleberry didn't commit what some called, crepe murder, pruning the beauties to practically nubs. The town let them grow at will, only trimming up the wild branches that blocked the way for town folk.

Henry Getty, the tallest man in town, petitioned for the higher branches to be trimmed when a rebel branch poked him in the eye and scratched his eyeball. Henry was six feet nine inches tall, so he'd offered to do the job himself, and the City Council members let him.

Every time I arrived at work, my heart skipped a beat, and I wanted to jump for joy. I loved my job, and I adored my office. The building itself was marked as a historical property in town, having received the honor several years prior to my coming to work there. The office was originally the home of Annabelle Castleberry, the daughter of the town's founder, Andrew Castleberry. She'd passed the stunning two story house, built in 1845, over to her children, and eventually it was donated to the city as a historical site and made the historical society's offices and museum.

The over five thousand square feet home was indeed a historic masterpiece. Andrew Castleberry wanted the best for his daughter, and paid attention to every detail, ensuring the home out classed every other one in town. It held all of the detailed work from the era including the tall ceilings, vast entry hall that was bigger than my kitchen and den combined, heart pine floors, and ornate trim work. The grand staircase, still the home's original, curved up to the second floor to the society's offices, while the first floor was used as the town museum.

I unlocked the door, flipped the sign on it to open, and closed the door behind me. Every morning I followed a specific path, flipping on the lights in each of the museum rooms first and then headed to the kitchen to fill my water bottle. As I did, I saw someone out of the corner of my eye in the main parlor area, but when I flipped on the light, the room was empty. My head ached, a low, dull pain very likely caused from a recent trip down the last few steps of those grand stairs, but I ignored it and carried on.

My assistant, though I preferred to call her coworker, because I honestly felt we were a team, Olivia Castleberry, a how many greats I wasn't sure, granddaughter of Andrew Castleberry, and a sweet young woman stood at the back counter in the kitchen preparing a pitcher of iced tea. "Hey, Miss Chantilly, you ready to hit the ground running today?"

I watched the water as it filled my bottle, making sure it didn't spill over the top. "I could be. Where are we running to?"

"You didn't get my text, did you?"

I retrieved my phone from my pocket. "I did, but I forgot to turn my phone volume on, so I didn't realize you'd sent something. Sorry about that." I read her text. "That's right, we're doing a meet and greet with some of the barbecue competition people today." The BBQ competition was just a few days away, and there was still a lot of work to do.

"And because you're one of the judges. You can't forget that. The judges always participate in the meet and greets."

Bless her heart, Olivia had all but forced me into being a judge. Olivia and I were like fraternal twins born nineteen years apart. I was the more organized, structured twin, and she was the flighty, spacey one. Except since the tumble, I felt like we'd switched roles. "I'll be ready, I promise."

She smiled. "I've already got our files ready. Yours is on your desk. There is a list of the committee heads, with a photograph and brief bio for each, a list of the most current applicants for the competition, which of course, I've also included photographs and short bios for, and the map of the layout for competition day."

I screwed the lid onto my water bottle. All that info sounded like overkill, but Olivia understood I'd been gone a long time, and she wanted to make sure I knew the people involved. "Wow Olivia, that's wonderful, thank you."

She dismissed my appreciation with an it was nothing hand wave and placed the pitcher in the refrigerator. "How're you feeling by the way?"

"I'm fine. It really wasn't anything." She worried about my tumble, and the lump the size of a walnut on the back of my head to show for it. It hurt, but not enough to warrant a trip to the doctor.

"Bless your heart, of course it was. You took a tumble down those stairs but good. I told you, you needed to go see Doc Bramblett. I don't know why you're so stubborn."

"I'm not stubborn. I'm busy. I have a pre-teen son, remember? He keeps me busy."

"I spent a lot of time around twelve-year-old boys, and I can tell you they one hundred percent did not want to be hanging with their momma's, so I'm not sure what he's got you doing that's keeping you so busy, but if that's your excuse, fine."

I shifted my eyes toward a basket of muffins on the counter, partially to avoid continuing the conversation, but also because I hadn't eaten breakfast at home or at the café, and I was starving.

Since my parents' deaths and my divorce, I've probably latched onto Austin more than I should. Our lives flipped upside down in a hot minute, twisted into a tight knot, and then bounced like a basketball in March Madness when my ex-husband decided to up and leave while we'd been at an overnight lacrosse tournament. Austin wasn't much of a communicator in general, but since the three hits to our hearts, he'd become a kid of few words, preferring to play lacrosse or video games when he had the chance. I'd done my best to give him every opportunity to express his feelings if he wanted, but so far, he hadn't. My daddy always said time heals all wounds, we just have to remember we can't rush time. I took that to heart when it came to Austin's grief. He'd lost a lot, and I wouldn't pressure him to be something he wasn't ready to be.

Like say, a kid with feelings. Then again, I didn't know one mother back in Birmingham that had a twelve-year-old son with emotions. It just wasn't their thing. I'd been working hard to adjust to the new little alien that had taken over my kid long before tragedy made him even more distant.

Arriving home to half of our houseful of furniture emptied, every single belonging of my husband, Scott's gone, and a note on the kitchen counter that read, I've met someone else resting on an envelope of divorce papers wasn't just hard on me, it tore Austin's heart to pieces. He may have not been able to express that, but it was apparent when, each time his father attempted to see him, he said no. I'd talked to experts and friends, and each suggested I give him my support and allow him to make his own decisions. Scott didn't like it, but I let karma do its thing because it wasn't my job to try and fix what he broke. I just wished karma hadn't picked my son as its chosen path.

What man leaves his child at such a crucial time of his life?

In hindsight, my turning around and moving back home probably wasn't the brightest move where Austin was concerned, but he seemed to be adjusting well. No longer faced with nearly daily drop ins by Scott took a load of stress and pressure off of him, and I'd seen him smile more in the past month than the several prior. I considered that a significant success.

"Miss Chantilly?"

I pivoted from the counter. "Yes?"

Olivia walked toward me and tilted her head as she smiled up at me. "Ma'am, you didn't hear a word I said, did you?"

"I'm sorry. I was off in divorce land again."

She huffed and rubbed my arm. "Oh honey, I just cannot imagine how that must have been. I am so grateful my parents have a good relationship. I don't know what it would be like to have to deal with divorce. Austin must be a wreck from it. And poor you. To lose the love of your life like that, it's just terrible." She shook her head. "Just terrible."

"Austin's a trouper. He's enjoying school, has made a lot of friends, and he's really enjoying being on the fall lacrosse team, so that's good."

"I'm glad. Now we just have to get you back on the team, too, the dating team." She grabbed a medium sized glass container of iced tea from the back deck, tossed a quarter bag of crushed ice into it, and shook it. The ice hit the bottle sides so hard my head throbbed. "There's nothing like a glass of fresh sun kissed sweet tea."

"Didn't you just put a thing of sweet tea in the 'fridge?"

"Well, yes, but that's for the patrons of the museum. It's good, but this is my family's secret tea recipe. It has to be outside for at least five full days of sunshine. By the way, I'm not sharing this with anyone but you." She poured herself a glass of the good stuff, and then set the container on the floor next to the counter. "Now, what can we do to get you back on that team I was talking about?"

"I'm not ready for that yet, and I'm not sure if I ever will be." I'd burned that bridge long ago.

"Maybe you aren't ready yet, but one day you will be, and we'll get you online or something and find you a good man."

"Let's table this conversation until I am ready, what do you think?"

"Miss Chantilly, as my daddy says, one day it'll be time to poop or get off the pot."

"I have a feeling your daddy doesn't say poop."

"Well heavens no, but a lady doesn't use foul language."

"Then I must not know that many ladies." I winked at her, and I snatched a chocolate, chocolate chip muffin from the basket on the counter and scooted on up to my office.

I sat at my desk and massaged the bump on the back of my head. It had hurt, tripping down the last few stairs of the Historical Society, but I couldn't bring myself to see Doc Bramblett. The last time I had was at my father's funeral. He'd offered his apologies, saying over and over how much he'd wished he could have helped Daddy, but the cancer was widespread and advanced so quickly that by the time my father went to him, it was too late to offer anything much more than comfort.

Yes, I saw the irony in that, but my situation was different. I'd fallen and hit my head. Daddy had cancer, and Parkinson's to boot, and that was entirely different than a knock on the noggin.

I wasn't upset with Doc. I knew he was right, that he couldn't help Daddy, and I didn't hold anything against the man, but even just thinking about that baby blue exam room in the doctor's home office brought back the horrible memories of the day Daddy and I got the news. We'd already lost Momma, and hearing I'd lose Daddy, too was unbearable. I'd stayed strong there for Daddy, but the office held memories I just didn't want to relive.

I distracted myself from the pain by printing out a copy of the new verbiage for Hamilton House's historical marker. The markers weren't iron plaques like in some towns, just script printed on fancy paper encased in a box near the main entrance, and sometimes inside depending on the location. They were easy to change out that way, and since I'd already changed seven in town, I was grateful.

First Holbrook Tyson, the town mayor would need to approve it, and then city officials would vote on it. I would mail a copy eventually, but I preferring dropping off an actual printed copy. It gave the mayor a feeling of what the finished product would look like, and usually worked in my favor. I'd planned to do that on the way back from the BBQ competition meeting.

I spent the rest of the forty minutes before we had to leave reviewing the contestant bios. It didn't surprise me that I didn't know many of the contestants, and I appreciated being able to read about them.

Olivia knocked on my open office door. "Come on in, sweetie," I said. I looked up, but she wasn't there. "Olivia?" Her feet pounded on the hardwood stairs, so I walked over to my office door and peeked out into the hallway. Olivia wasn't in sight. "You could have come in, you weren't disturbing me." I didn't have to holler because my voice echoed through the grand entry.

She popped out from one of the rooms on the left side at the bottom of the stairs and cocked her eyebrow. "Excuse me, Miss Chantilly? Did you say something to me?"

"I said you could have come in, you didn't even need to knock."

She tipped her head sideways. "I'm not sure what you're sayin'."

I swung my head from side to side, glancing around me in

case it was someone else, someone that had come in without a sound. "You were just up here a second ago, weren't you?"

She shook her head. "No, ma'am. I've been straightening up the new exhibit like you asked me to before the weekend." She pressed her lips together. "Would you like me to go ahead and make that appointment with Doc Bramblett for you?"

"I'm fine, but thank you. I had my head buried in the bios, so I must have imagined it." I could have sworn she knocked on my door. Funny, the night before, I could have also sworn Austin was clanging pots and pans in the kitchen, but he was in the den with his headphones on playing some video games. It was the weirdest thing, but he promised he hadn't just been in the kitchen, and I believed him.

Both rooms were on opposite ends of the house. I'd called to him from my bedroom, but he ignored me, so I stomped through the house like an angry mother only to find him in the den with his earbuds glued to the insides of his ears. He argued that he hadn't been in the kitchen since we'd cleaned up after dinner. Since it was the only night he didn't have fall league lacrosse practice and the only opportunity he had to play video games, I believed him.

I'd checked the kitchen thinking perhaps one of the pots had fallen from the pot rack, but they were all still hanging there, so I figured I'd imagined it.

Again.

"Miss Chantilly?"

"What? No, no. I'm fine, really."

"Sweetie pie, I just asked you that question twice, and you didn't hear a word."

I furrowed my brow. "You did not."

She nodded. "I sure did."

"Well, I heard you once, so that's something." I breathed out a frustrated sigh. "I've just got a lot on my mind at the moment, that's all. If my head doesn't get any better soon, I'll make my appointment. You're an employee of the historical society, not my personal assistant."

"I know, but I'm happy to help."

"And I appreciate that."

I gathered my things, and we walked over to Hamilton House for the meeting. It was only a few blocks up the main road on the opposite end of downtown Castleberry, which wasn't much longer than a horse's tail and the hominess of the small town was exactly what I'd run home to when my divorce was finalized. That and the fact that my parents had left me their house, and Austin and I needed a place to live.

Olivia introduced me to the few contestants that had shown up for the meeting and were a small part of the planning committee. Their part was small because we didn't want to give anyone ammunition to say we'd favored a competitor because they'd helped plan the event. Mostly they were just there to make sure we had everything the contestants needed for a fair competition. Since it was my first year running the thing, I needed the help. When the original committee head left the position two months ago, I gladly took it. The busier, the better, I'd thought. Instead I'd ended up overwhelmed and exhausted.

"You already know Bobby Joe Pruitt, obviously," she said.

I smiled. "Of course. We graduated from high school together."

Her eyes sparkled. "Oh, how did I not know that?" She grabbed hold of Bobby Joe's arm and squeezed. "You do know Miss Chantilly here is single again, don't you?"

I looked away, not because I was embarrassed, but because I didn't want either of them to see the horror in my eyes. If ever I did plan to date, it wouldn't be Bobby Joe Pruitt. His reputation had always been sketchy, and he wasn't the kindest man in town. I knew Castleberry was small, and the pickings were slim, but if I did decide to date again, I could just as easily head over to Alpharetta or something south of us where the options were better. I saw none of that happening though, and I kept my thoughts to myself.

Bobby's ears turned red, which wasn't hard to notice. He wasn't trying to hide them, and even if he tried, he couldn't. His bald head showed the world his red ears and bumpy skull. "I did have a crush on you back in the day."

Olivia's smile stretched from one side of her face almost to the other side of the restaurant. "Oh, isn't that just the sweetest thing? I can get you two a reservation up at the Honky Tonk Bar and Grill if you'd like." She wiggled her eyebrows. "Best catfish in town."

I'd never liked catfish, so I just smiled and said thank you, but my schedule was full at that moment. If she tried to play Cupid again, I'd have to have a talk with her about it.

Bobby laughed. "That would be mighty nice, but I'm seeing me someone now, and I think it's going to be serious right quick."

Olivia gasped. "Excuse me, Mr. Bobby Joe Pruitt, you're seeing someone? Who is the lucky girl?"

"We ain't telling nobody just yet. She's fixin' to end a bad relationship, and we don't want no trouble before she does."

"Oh, well, bless her heart. I hope she can do that right quick." Olivia smiled at me. "We'll just find Miss Chantilly here someone else when the time is right."

The time was not right, and the someone was most definitely not Bobby Joe Pruitt. I kind of felt a little sorry for the person he dated. Bobby smelled like he hadn't showered in days. "That's wonderful, Bobby. I hope it works out for you."

Rashid Patel shook my hand. "Nice to meet you. My family recipe will win this year's competition. My secret ingredient is from my great grandmother in India. You will like it very much."

"I'm sure I will," I said.

Bobby Joe grunted. His sweet disposition flipped upside down. "Good barbecue don't need no secret from across the world, and Castleberry sure don't need you taking over the old Barton Family Restaurant space neither. That barbecue ain't gonna sell like you think."

"My food is much liked in this community, and my current restaurant location cannot accommodate the many people that want to eat my special recipe barbecue. I do not understand why you must continue to offer upsetting complications to my business," Rashid said. His English wasn't entirely choppy, but I could tell he struggled to choose his words.

Delphina walked over and swatted Bobby on the back of the head. "Bobby Joe Pruitt, put a sock in it." Del could treat Bobby that way. She and his mother had been close friends until Eugena Pruitt died four years ago, and Del was the only family, blood related or not, he had left.

Bobby rubbed the back of his head. "Dagnumit Del, you don't gotta hit me like that."

"If you'd behave, I wouldn't have to. Besides, you know I promised your momma I'd keep you from acting like a fool, don't make me break that promise, you hear?"

Poor Bobby Joe Pruitt. He wasn't the most popular guy in town. In fact, most people couldn't stand him, but they forgave him his transgressions because he made the best BBQ around.

Maybelle Parker, Bobby's main cook, waddled into the main dining area from the kitchen. Maybelle liked to sample the food, a lot, hence the waddle. Her chipper personality fit her short, stout stature, and everyone loved her. I'd never once seen Maybelle in a bad mood. "Bobby, got a sec? There's a little problem with the ovens."

Bobby dropped his chin to his chest and sighed. "I hired a bunch of idiots. 'Cuse me." He stepped through the kitchen door, but not before telling us to take a seat in the private dining area on our right. "I'll be done right quick."

We walked into the room, our entrance surprising a younger couple standing near one of the tables. The woman glanced down at something on the table and hurried to stuff it into her bag. I recalled seeing them around town, but I hadn't met them personally, though I was pretty sure they owned the food truck often parked at the lacrosse fields.

Olivia introduced us. "Miss Chantilly, this is Jesse and Julia Lye. They moved to Castleberry about four years ago." She smiled at the couple. "You probably know their food truck, Lye BBQ? It's at all the town events and is usually parked over by the sports park on weekends." She smiled at the couple. "Miss Chantilly is the director of the historical society. She just moved back to town because her husband left her." She leaned toward them and whispered, "But she doesn't like to talk much about that."

I wanted to roll my eyes, but I just smiled and took the hit. Olivia meant well. Sometimes she just lacked tact. "It's a pleasure to meet you. I just had a barbecue sandwich from your food truck last weekend. It was incredible."

Jesse stood, his ample belly jiggling as he shook my hand. His smile was hearty and genuine, and his burly, teddy bear look hollered true Southerner. I instantly liked him. It was hard to describe because it wasn't about appearance as much as facial features and actions. Julia, on the other hand, wasn't from the south. Her Northeastern appearance gave that away. Birmingham was a hot spot for transients from Pennsylvania and New Jersey, and Julia reminded me of my friends from there. She pulled her long, dyed blacker than black hair back in a tight ponytail at the top of her head, and the color of her thick black eyeliner framing her eyes matched it perfectly. When she shook my hand, her long, bright green nail tips dug into my palm.

Jesse's, "Hey, nice to meetcha," exuded a powerful Southern drawl.

Julia's, "Hi," meant she hadn't lived in the south long.

I sat in a seat facing the main dining room, and I kept my eyes glued to the doorway. The private room initially served as the parlor and was the perfect spot for formal parties and meetings, but I had a thing about small rooms, so facing the door always gave me comfort. Though my positioning was good for my claustrophobic tendencies, it also gave me a perfect view of the area where Agnes Hamilton hanged herself years before.

As a kid that area gave me goosebumps, but my older self knew it was just an old town tale.

The restaurant hostess, a teenager from the local high school, offered us all sweet tea or Coke. I asked for a coffee instead, as did Rashid and Del.

My eyes followed her as she walked out of the entrance, and I thought about poor Agnes. For years people have claimed to see her spirit in her old house, most often in the very foyer where, wearing her beautifully beaded wedding gown, she took her life.

Agnes never got the chance to wear the dress in her actual wedding because her fiancé ran off and left her for another woman days before. I cringed at the small similarity in our lives.

Some people claimed to see her spirit wandering through the kitchen or other dining areas, and a few people reported seeing her in the upstairs windows at night, but I never had, and I didn't really believe ghosts were real anyway, but I could admit to being curious. I just assumed if she'd stuck around, she'd make her presence obvious. I knew I would.

I stared out into the foyer as Olivia made small talk with the contestants, and I swore I caught a glimpse of a white beaded train scoot across the floor. The mind had an amazing way of playing tricks on people, didn't it? I shook my head and refocused on the casual conversation at the table.

Del caught my eye and mouthed, "Are you okay?"

I nodded.

The hostess came back with our drinks and placed a basket of fresh biscuits in the middle of the table. Bobby and Maybelle followed behind her. Bobby's face was red and sweaty, and I couldn't help but hope he didn't drip any of that sweat into his food. I pressed my eyes shut to clear the thought from my head. I glanced down at the biscuits and suddenly had no desire to eat.

Bobby blinked and pointed his chubby finger between Jesse and Julia. "What in God's name are these two doing here?" His voice grew louder with each word. "They ain't allowed in my business establishment." He grabbed Maybelle by the shoulder. "You let these two crooks in?"

Del stood and placed a calming hand on Bobby's arm. "They're key contestants in the competition, Bobby. You know that. They came to help finalize the to-do list for the event."

Julia stood and walked a circle around the table next to us, running her hand along the place settings.

Bobby's face burned hotter than the late summer sun, and he snatched up the couple's sweet teas and handed them back to the hostess. "I don't care if they're the President of the United States. They ain't allowed in my restaurant." He rubbed the top of his head and growled toward the hostess who'd attempted to quietly sneak out of the room. "You know they was here?"

The poor girl stuttered as she spoke. "Yes, sir, but I…I thought you were okay with it seein' as they came with Miss Delphina and all."

He grabbed the basket of biscuits she'd placed on the table and threw it across the room.

Well, darn. There went any chance at having one if I'd changed my mind. The biscuits hit the wall all at once, dropped to the old wood planked floor, and stuck.

"Git outta my restaurant." He shook his finger at the couple and then at Rashid. "And you, too. All y'all come here like you're trying to take over our town with your food trucks and your funny tasting barbecue restaurants, and don't nobody want you here. Nobody."

Del grabbed hold of Bobby's arm again and hissed in his ear. "Bobby Joe Pruitt, shut up. That's the devil talking through you."

"I ain't having no meeting with people trying to ruin my business."

Jesse stood and slammed his palms onto the table. "We haven't done a thing to you. You're the one that's caused the rift between us, coming to the park and sticking that food cart up next to our truck like that."

"Without a permit," Julia added.

I swallowed a sip of my coffee. I didn't want to rubberneck on their argument, but it was impossible not to.

"I had me a permit," Bobby said.

"Yeah, weeks later, and only because you've got connections with the city council," she said.

"That permit was retroactivated. I didn't do nothing wrong."

My English degree kicked in, and I almost corrected Bobby's mispronounced word, but I didn't dare poke the bear.

Del interrupted apologies to everyone and suggested we continue the meeting via email or a later get together attempt. "I'm ashamed of Bobby's behavior." She shot a steely stare at the man. "I realize he's not kin, but he's like kin, and I feel responsible for him." She dragged Bobby away by his left earlobe.

"Ouch, Del. Don't pinch so hard."

Julia set her purse on the table behind ours. "Is it appropriate for her to be a judge in this competition when she's personally involved with someone like this?"

Olivia raised her hand. "Excuse me, may I speak?"

"You don't need approval," I said. "Go ahead."

"Thank you, Miss Chantilly." She centered her eyes straight onto Julia Lye's. "Miss Delphina here has been a judge in the competition for years. She's never once been swayed by her relationship with Bobby Pruitt, and you should know that your very self since you've won the competition before."

Julia didn't respond. She just raised the side of her lip, dipped the edges of her eyebrows in at her nose, and jiggled her head.

"It was nice formally meetin' ya," Jesse said. He shook my

hand. "It think I ought to get my wife out of here now. She's got her momma's Italian temper."

"That man could bring out the devil in the nicest person," she said.

Rashid Patel suggested I come by his restaurant again and try his secret family recipe BBQ prior to the competition, promising me I would love it. I told him I wasn't comfortable with doing that so close to the competition. I suspected the secret ingredient was curry, which was one of my all time favorite seasonings, and I really wanted to try them, but I didn't feel it would be right.

Olivia and I packed up our things to leave, but Delphina asked me to stay. "I have a quick favor."

"No problem." I asked Olivia to drop off the new copy for Hamilton House at the Mayor's office, gave her the file, and sent her on her way. I knew Mayor Holbrook would have questions, but I also knew I probably wouldn't hear back from him until after the BBQ competition.

As I waited in the private eating area, I thought about Agnes Hamilton again. I hoped I did her justice with the new verbiage for the historic home. "You deserve to be remembered for your strengths, not your last moments," I whispered toward the door.

A white cloud drifted in front of me and then immediately disappeared. I jumped out of my seat and headed straight toward the door as Del walked through it. I pointed in the direction of where the cloud disappeared. "Did you see that?"

Del's eyes followed my finger. "See what?"

I shook my head. "The white cloud. It was just… nothing, never mind."

Her smile wavered. "You probably should make a pit stop over at Doc Bramblett's on your way back to the office. You're not yourself since you bopped your head on the stairs."

"I'm fine. And it was the marble floor, actually."

She smirked. "Surprised the floor didn't crack from that big thing."

I harrumphed. "Thanks. I feel better now."

She laughed. "I hate to do this to you, but Bobby wants to make some changes to the restaurant, and I promised him I'd get you to take a look after the meeting. I just didn't expect the meeting to end like it did, but I think I got him cooled off now."

Since I was the head of the historical society, it was my job to review requests for changes made by owners of historic properties. The town had very explicit requirements for its historical buildings, many of which were pushed aggressively to be followed by the state, but we had a bit of wiggle room. Each was examined in great detail, partially because it was my job but also because I had a lot of late nights free since I wasn't spending them with my husband, and if necessary, put to vote with the historical committee. "Not a problem. Just so you know, I've reviewed Hamilton House's file, and I know he's made requests before, but they've never been approved. I can't say this one will be, either."

She nodded. "I know, but I appreciate you letting him show you." She led me past the stairs to the cellar by the back entrance to the home and toward the kitchen.

I quickly glanced behind me, just wondering if that white cloud was still floating around, but it wasn't.

Bobby's requests were a bit off the wall, but I understood his reasoning behind them. "I'm just not sure this is in line with our historic property guidelines, but I'll do a thorough review and let you know."

"Last year Billy Price got his place redone, and it's a historic location. Not sure why my changes don't never get approved."

His face reddened like it had earlier, and I feared I'd be the brunt of his anger like the others.

Del attempted to soften his rudeness. "Now Bobby, you promised me you wouldn't get out of sorts about this if I asked Chantilly to come talk to you, remember?"

He wiggled that pointer finger at me, obviously that was what he did when he felt defensive. "She ain't even been in town a hot minute, and she thinks she can make decisions about historical evaluations on our businesses? Don't know why they gave her the job."

"I grew up here, remember? And this isn't my first trip to the rodeo, Bobby. I know what I'm doing." And I did. I'd worked with the historic society in Birmingham for several years. My experience far outweighed the need in Castleberry, and the lighter work load was exactly what I needed at that time in my life, other than the long, lonely nights when I had time to think, at least.

Maybelle stepped into the small office. "Bobby, the oven's done acting up again. Should I do that thing you showed me?"

He threw the rolled up plans I'd asked for at his office door. They sailed past me making a whooshing sound. "Why you got to ask me that? Just do it."

Del marched over to his side of the desk and grabbed him by the earlobe again. I cringed. My momma used to do that to me when I was a kid and it hurt like a son of a gun. "Bobby Joe Pruitt, you have got to get a hold of this temper of yours, you hear me? If you don't kill yourself from a heart attack, someone in town's going to do it, and I got a feeling it'll be me."

Delphina's face was almost as red as Bobby's. She breathed in loudly, letting the breath out in one full shot, and then she focused on me. "Don't know how such a sweet woman like his momma ended up with a tyrant like this."

I wasn't sure, but if there was one thing I was certain of, it was that one of my life's goals would be to never do anything that would garner me an earlobe drag by Delphina Beauregard.

"You done acting like a fool?" she asked him.

He narrowed his eyes at me while he breathed through a clenched but opened jaw. "You get outta here, too, Chantilly. Don't know what I ever saw in you back in the day, but I sure don't see nothing but a dried up old pile of garbage now. Don't need the likes of you in my restaurant either."

I stood. "Bobby, you certainly don't deserve my effort, but since it's my job, I'll do what I'm required to do, and I'll do it to the best of my ability. I suggest however, you tamper that temper of yours and act like the forty-five-year-old man you are instead of some kind of spoiled brat."

"Can't make sugar from salt," Delphina said.

I apologized to her, and she to me, and then I left. As I walked out of the small office and down the stairs of the old home, I froze.

There, swinging from a rope tied around a rafter in the main dining area, hung Agnes Hamilton. I saw her with my very own eyes, and I knew within the pit of my soul she wasn't in my head.

CHAPTER 2

*L*acrosse practice lasted thirty minutes longer than usual because the coach wanted to make sure the boys knew the plays backwards, forwards, sideways, and upside down for their first game of the season. I sat in the bleachers reviewing Bobby's plans as the sun's warm amber glow set below the horizon.

"Is that Hamilton House?" Lonna Appleton scooted up next to me.

Lonna and I went way back, but I'd never once considered her a friend. We weren't exactly enemies, though back in our high school days there were times it sure felt that way. Looking back with a mature eye, I realized it was more jealousy than anything. Lonna came from a family that spoiled their children with the newest and greatest buys—which, back then, were things like Nike high tops, leather bomber jackets and Ray ban sunglasses—and that in turn, gave them a monumental sense of entitlement that stretched to everything they did.

We'd both tried out for the cheerleading squad and made it, but I received the captain spot, and Lonna pitched a fit because of the unfairness of it all. Determined the title belonged to her, she went to the principal and said I'd mistreated her, making her a base for stunts when she was far too thin for such a powerful position. She thought she should be a fly like I was.

I was a whopping five feet two inches and one hundred pounds back then, and Lonna trumped me by at least five inches and twenty pounds. Tossing her into the air would have broken our backs. She wasn't heavy by any means, but in cheerleading, the smallest girls were the tossers—the ones tossed, officially called the fly position, not the larger ones. The principal saw my side of things, and the argument ended with her ugly crying her Dial A Lash mascara all over her face.

We also competed for the president of student council, and I'd won. It wasn't that I was more popular, because I wasn't. It wasn't that I was smarter, because I wasn't. It was that I worked harder, and that hard work paid off.

And the entitlement thing probably had a lot to do with it, too. Kids raised in Castleberry weren't typically entitled. We were lucky to have what we did, but Lonna's family had money, and that mattered to them.

"Yes," I smiled as I made eye contact. "He's looking to do some reno on the place, so I'm reviewing the architect's plans." I gazed out onto the turf lacrosse field just in time to see my son finish his part of a play. "What brings you here?"

Lonna had two children, both of which were girls, so I couldn't see a reason for her to attend an all boys lacrosse team practice.

"Oh, haven't you heard?" She flipped her long black hair behind her.

"Heard what?"

"Coach Jack and I are dating. Have been for the past three months. I figured someone would have mentioned it by now. Lord knows the entire town is talking about it."

Maybe so, but they weren't talking about it to me. Not that I cared anyway, but in an effort to bury the long held hatchet, I faked my excitement for her. She'd always had a thing for Jack Levitt. "Oh, that's great news. Congratulations. Wait, didn't y'all date in high school for a bit?" Okay, so that just flew out of my mouth before I could stop it

Her smile wavered, but only for a moment. "Oh, yes, but we were so young then. Things have a way of working themselves out, and the time is right now, it just wasn't then."

If I remembered correctly, and I was pretty sure I did, Jack Levitt broke up with her a few months into their relationship. I didn't know the reason then, and I didn't much care still. "Well, good for you. I hope it works out for you."

"Oh sweetie, I can tell you for certain it will. They don't make men like Jack anymore. Bless his heart, I think he's the last true Southern gentlemen from our era."

"That's great." I wasn't exactly sure what she wanted me to say.

"I just wish he'd quit that job of his. It's so dangerous. Daddy's company would hire him on the spot, but he says he's got no interest in building homes." She rolled her eyes. "Don't know why. The market is booming. Why Daddy just bought two hundred acres south of here. He's planning on building another three hundred or more homes in the next six months. Jack would be busier than a bee managing a crew."

I just smiled. I couldn't argue Coach Jack's decisions, I'd barely talked to him about anything other than lacrosse since moving back to town.

"Oh, and I just can't believe Bobby's still trying to get those plans approved. You read my article on Hamilton House a few months back, right? It was one of the special historic features I do every now and again. He mentioned them to me, too. I love that old home. It's just beautiful, and the history is to die for."

"I must have missed that." I snuck a look at Jack as he spoke to the boys on the field. His broad shoulders, strong, trim physique, and salt and pepper hair cut close to his head didn't say construction manager, but they screamed ex-Marine and police detective, which is exactly what he was. Jack headed the investigative division of our small police department. I suspected it wasn't a hard job because Castleberry, Georgia didn't have a whole lot of crime to speak of. But from what I understood, he'd done it for several years, so maybe it was because of him. Maybe he'd been doing something right. "About the job of Jack's. A man's going to do what he thinks is best. We can't change them, now, can we?"

"Well, maybe you can't, but I can, and I intend to get that hunk of a military man out of uniform for good. It's just too dangerous these days, what with the state of our world now, don't you think?"

I nodded because I knew if I said anything different she'd push back even harder, and I just didn't have the energy or desire to verbally spar with the likes of Lonna Appleton. Twenty or so years ago I would have been all over that, but not anymore. I'd learned to pick and choose my battles, and none of them included Lonna Appleton.

Thankfully Jack blew his whistle signaling the end of practice, and the boys hollered their team chant. I gathered my things and put them in my bag. "Well, time to feed the monster. You're lucky you have girls. My kid eats like food grows on trees."

She stared at me. "Doesn't some of it?"

"That was sarcasm, Lonna."

I met Austin at the entrance to the field as he walked over with Coach Jack.

Jack smiled at me, and his hazel eyes sparkled with little sprinkles of gold around his irises. I'd never noticed that before. "Hey, got a minute?"

I glanced behind me and saw Lonna staring at us with a familiar gaze I immediately recognized from years past. "Uh, sure?" I handed Austin the keys to the car. "Toss your stuff in back, and open the windows. I don't need that stink of yours infiltrating my lungs. I'd like to get us both home safely before it kills me."

He grunted something and walked away.

Jack smirked. "They do stink, don't they?"

"To high heaven, as my momma used to say." The flash of that small memory pinched my heart, but I held it together. I'd learned not to show those emotions to people because it always made them uncomfortable. No one knew how to handle other people's grief, especially the grief of people who'd lost such important people so close together. Grief was painful enough without the added awkwardness of those who'd yet to experience it.

Jack's smile softened. "I'm really sorry about your parents. They were good people."

"Thank you."

"Listen, I know you've been going through some things, and I'm sure it's all been tough on Austin, too."

Anxiety was my immediate response to the unknown, and I immediately wanted to cut and run. If given the chance to fight or fly lately, I chose fly. I'd done enough fighting over the past year to last a lifetime, and I just didn't have it in me any longer. I tapped my foot to tame the urge. "Is something going on? Did he say something to you?"

"Oh, no, no. He hasn't said a thing. I just figured it's been hard on him. But if he, you know, needs someone to talk to, other than you, I mean, I'm here. I just wanted to let you know."

I let out a breath I'd been holding in. "I appreciate that, Coach, thank you. He could use a good male figure in his life. He and my ex aren't on the best of terms at the moment."

He nodded. "I understand. If you'd like, I'll mention that I'm here for him at practice tomorrow. You never know what might happen."

"That would be nice. Thank you."

"And Chantilly, we grew up together. You don't have to call me Coach, you know that, right?"

I smiled. "Of course, Coach, I mean Jack. I know that."

Yes, we'd grown up together, but our friendship was years ago, and with the time I'd been gone added to that, Jack felt like a stranger to me.

As I walked to my car, I glanced behind me and saw Coach, or Jack, shake his head and walk away with Lonna trailing behind him. I had a feeling she was giving him a lecture about me, and I couldn't help but smile.

L iving in my childhood home as an adult gave me a unique perspective on the home itself. My parents renovated the early 1900s ranch several times, at one point even adding a second story for the master bedroom. Years later they added a wall for a bathroom addition because my mother tired of going down the stairs three times a night to go to the bathroom. At my age I was just starting to understand how much of an annoyance that could have been.

Momma loved antiques and had a knack for choosing time-less pieces that easily intermixed with any décor, so I'd kept many of their belongings. I wanted to purge everything having anything to do with my marriage to Scott—except my son, of course—when we moved, but the life change wasn't just mine, and to make things easier on and more familiar for Austin, I brought a lot of it with us.

The old house was quiet at night, sometimes so quiet I could almost hear the memories whisper through the rooms. After Austin went to bed, I tidied up, finished washing his lacrosse clothing and sprayed Lysol into his lacrosse bag before setting it on the back porch. I refused to leave that sickly sweet smelling mass in the house. I didn't want the smell permeating the walls. If it rained, it had a place in the garage of course, but I figured it was a good wild animal repellent out on the porch. Castleberry had a coyote and bobcat issue, though I hadn't seen either myself yet, and I swore that was because of the wretched stench of the bag.

I brought Bobby's architect plans upstairs and laid them out on my bed. My Burmese cat jumped up and stretched out on top of the rolled out papers. "Cooper, seriously? I'm reading those."

Not surprisingly, he completely ignored me. I gently pushed him off but he scooched right back into the same spot. Before I had a chance to pick him up again, something on the opposite side of the room caught his eye. He crouched into his hunting cat position and darted off the papers toward the edge of my bed. He whipped his head back and forth, and I watched with a careful eye. "Coopie, whatcha see?" I patted his back but he paid no attention. "Coopie?"

He kept his eyes focused across the room. Knowing my cat, it could have been a speckle of dust caught in the reflection of the moon shining through my blinds. He stretched his left leg out toward the window, meowed, and then, as cats so often did, lost interest, turned around and splayed back out over Bobby's redesign plans.

I swooped him up under my arm and carried him down to Austin's room. "Okay, that's it. You can go stretch across Austin for now."

He meowed as I closed the door behind me. I didn't feel bad. He preferred Austin over me anyway and had made that perfectly clear time and time again.

As I walked back toward the stairs, a voice came from in the kitchen. I froze. I knew Austin was in bed. I just laid eyes on him. No one else was inside. I certainly would have heard them come in, unless of course they were there before we got home, and they'd been hiding. Sure, it was unlikely, but it wasn't impossible. I tiptoed as lightly as possible toward the kitchen and listened intently.

There it was again. A soft laugh with a high pitched squeak at the end. A laugh I knew better than any other. "Momma?" I nixed the tiptoeing and bolted to the kitchen. I flipped on the overhead light but there was no one there. I scolded myself for thinking and wishing, for hoping Momma would be standing at the counter sipping a cup of coffee and laughing at something Daddy said.

They were dead. I knew they were dead, and I had grown to accept being an adult orphan, but every once in a while, my mind played tricks on me. Sometimes I just wanted the last year to be a terrible nightmare—the divorce, my parents' death, all of it. Okay, maybe not the divorce because Scott's true character hit me like a brick, and I wouldn't take him back knowing what I knew, no matter what, but the rest, yes, that I wished was a terrible nightmare.

I gave myself a pep talk as I climbed back up the stairs. Of course I'd think I could hear my parents. It was their home. Their lives, their memories, their souls were imprinted into the walls, the floors, the very heart of the home. It was filled with their energy. That gave me peace of mind and helped to heal my broken heart most of the time. Sometimes though, it made me sad and yearn for something I'd never have again.

I sulked up the stairs and got to work. I reviewed Bobby's architectural plans and noted some suggestions then rolled up the papers and stuffed them back into the tube. Even though he'd been rude, I still had a job to do, and I intended to do it. His requested changes weren't too much to ask, and I didn't think they would be a problem for the historic committee to approve, at least not with some minor revisions.

. . .

I dropped Austin off at school and stopped at Community Café for a large coffee to bring to work. Del apologized again for Bobby's behavior.

"Delphina, you do not have to apologize. I know you feel an obligation to his mother, but he's a grown man, and if he doesn't get it by now, there's nothing you can do to change that. He's just going to have to figure it out himself. Or not. Either way, you don't owe me any apology."

She smiled as she shrugged. "You're right, but I feel like I'm breaking my promise if I don't help the boy."

"He's not a boy. He's a forty-five-year-old man, and I doubt his momma would be defending him as much as you have. She'd probably whip his butt with a switch."

She laughed. "She probably would."

"Well, there you go."

We both laughed. I added cream to my coffee and headed to the office.

Just before nine o'clock I called Bobby's restaurant and left a message on voicemail that I'd be there shortly with the suggested changes to his plan. I really felt if he and the architect could agree, the committee would vote to approve the changes, and he could get started on the reno. I just hoped he saw it the same way.

I typed up a summary of the suggestions, enclosed them in an envelope, and locked up as I left. Olivia would arrive in a little under thirty minutes, but I never left the museum unlocked when it was empty. It wasn't that I didn't trust people, it was just a practice I'd grown accustomed to in Birmingham.

I smiled at Maybelle Parker as she headed toward me on the sidewalk. From the determination in her gait and the swing of her arms, I knew she was upset.

"Is everything okay, Maybelle? I'm headed to Hamilton House to drop these plans off with Bobby. Shouldn't you be heading that way, too?"

Her nostrils flared. "Have fun with that. I don't plan to go there ever again."

Bobby's temper must have struck again. "Oh, no. I'm sorry. Did something happen?"

She crossed her arms and stomped her foot. "That jerk fired me."

"No. I can't believe that. You're too valuable to him."

She nodded. "After all these years of doing the best I could for that good for nothing jerk, he ups and fires me because I'm trying to make something of myself."

"What did he say?"

She rolled her eyes. "He's just mad because I entered the barbecue competition yesterday and he found out. Said it's unethical to compete against your boss because I have an edge, what with knowing his barbecue recipe and all." She shook her head. "As if I'd ever use his recipe. Mine is ten times better than his, and he knows it. That's why he fired me. He's scared I'll beat him like those food truck people did last year."

I used a soft voice to try and calm her. "Maybelle, I'm so sorry. I know you're upset, but you know how Bobby is. He gets bent out of shape, pitches a fit, and then he's fine. Give him a few hours. I'm sure he'll be begging you to come back."

Her voice shook. "I don't care. I'm done working for that snake in the grass. He can drop dead for all I care."

I picked a bad time to bring him the plans, but then again, I wasn't sure there was ever really a good time where Bobby Pruitt was concerned.

Her hands whipped and swung all kinds of directions as she spoke. "If I was you, I'd turn around and march right back to the museum and rip up those papers. He don't deserve any kind of acceptance. He ought to just sell the place and settle somewhere else."

I wasn't quite sure if I should respond to that. I didn't want to upset her further, but I had a job to do. It didn't matter. She took a breath and then kept on venting.

"I got to go. I'm going straight to the bank and taking out a loan to open my own restaurant. A friend and me, we've been tossing the idea around for months now. I'm finally doing it. I don't have a thing to lose now, do I?" She marched off so I figured she didn't actually want an answer to her question, not that I had an answer anyway.

I stood there for a moment debating if it was the right time to bring the plans over to Bobby. He was probably boiling hot, and I was likely one of the last people he'd want to see, but I still had a job to do. It wasn't personal, and I had to handle it that way, too.

The front door was unlocked even though it was too early for lunch. I stepped inside and my shoes echoed on the old wood floor. I glanced up at the rafters as I always did. I thought I did it to honor Agnes, but a part of me wanted to catch a glimpse of her like so many others claimed to.

A cold breeze swished by me and sent a tingling chill up my back. I rubbed my bare arms and moved quickly toward the kitchen.

Two cooks were scrambling around, and I knew they were feeling Maybelle's loss. "Is Bobby here?" I asked.

Neither of them looked up from their stations, but one did say, "Try his office upstairs."

I headed up there, sneaking another peek at the rafter as I did. Agnes was nowhere to be found. Maybe yesterday was my imagination after all? Lord knows I'd thought about her enough in that short time to imagine her as she died. Maybe that's what everyone did, imagined her there and thought for sure she was real.

Bobby's office door was closed, so I knocked softly. "Bobby, it's Chantilly Adair. I have your plans, and they look pretty good. I just have a few things I'd like you to think about and we can submit them for review."

He didn't respond.

I tapped on the door again. "Bobby?"

When I got no answer again, I tried the handle. It twisted, so I took a chance and opened the door.

Bobby was there all right, but there was a reason he wasn't answering. He couldn't. He sat slumped in his chair behind his desk with a blackhandled knife protruding from his back.

"Bobby?" I rushed over to him and checked his pulse. "Oh, no. Bobby." I quickly hollered for help and grabbed the phone on his desk, dialing nine-five-five twice before my fingers finally got the number right.

The operator said she'd stay on the line, but I told her it wasn't necessary. She argued and suggested I leave the room, but I just couldn't leave poor Bobby like that. I stood and waited for the police to arrive, my heart racing and my head pounding, and my phone stuffed in my back pocket.

The small bedroom/office walls closed in on me. I struggled to breathe, and my temples throbbed. The room spun, and I felt faint.

Someone dressed in black barged in. I heard voices. They sounded mad, but I couldn't make out any words. A white cloud circled around me, and a woman screamed and cried off in the distance.

Frozen in place, my body heavy and cold, all I wanted to do was move, to run, but I couldn't. My feet were stuck to the ground, held by invisible weights so heavy I couldn't move. I blinked over and over, trying desperately to focus, but the room was too dark, too blurry, and I couldn't make out anything but shadowy images.

A white cloud.

A person dressed in black.

A rope.

A knife.

A letter dropping to the ground.

A deep guttural scream.

And then darkness.

"Chantilly? Chantilly, wake up." Strong hands gripped my shoulders and shook me, making my head throb more. "Wake up."

I opened my eyes slowly. "What's going on?" The fog cleared, and I stared Jack Levitt in the eyes. "There you are." He let go of my shoulders and helped me up. "You okay?"

I was a bit shaky, but I was fine, and I told him that. "What happened?"

"That's what I'd like to know. You called 911 and said Bobby Pruitt was dead. When we got here, you were passed out on the floor."

I rubbed the bump on the back of my head. It still hurt. "I passed out? Like fell on my face passed out?"

He shook his head. "More like the fetal position." He walked me out of the room and hollered to a police officer a few feet away. "Carter, take her to the paramedics and have her checked out, okay?" He smiled at me, a deep sincerity settling in his eyes. "Let them take care of you. I'll be out in a bit, okay?"

I nodded, and the officer helped me down the stairs.

The paramedics checked my vitals, though I assured them I was fine. They offered me a blanket and a bottled water, but I refused, eager to get back inside and see what was going on.

I stood outside of the historic building and waited for Jack to come out. It took him a good thirty minutes, and in that time a crowd had gathered. They hounded the two officers blocking the entrance.

"What's goin' on in there?"

"Was it a fire? I swore I heard a loud boom last night. Has to be a fire."

There wasn't even a smidgen of smoke rising from the building.

"Anyone hurt?"

I kept quiet. Jack came out and spoke briefly to the crowd as I stood by the ambulance, watching.

He kindly suggested they leave, saying their presence was a hindrance to the investigation, and most of the crowd dispersed but for a few stragglers sticking around, hoping to get their eyes on the action.

Jack nodded toward me as he walked up to the paramedics. "I'm going to need y'all to remove the deceased from the back side of the building. I'd like to give Bobby a little privacy."

"Yes, sir," both paramedics said.

"We'll give you the go ahead in a bit."

They nodded.

He leaned up against the ambulance. "How're you feeling?"

"A little shaky, but I'm okay."

"Tell me what happened."

I reiterated the events leading up to finding Bobby stabbed in his chair.

"Was anyone else in the office?"

"I don't think so."

"Do you remember how you ended up on the floor?"

Beads of sweat formed on my temples as I searched for an answer. "I don't know. It was really odd. One minute I'm on the phone with the emergency operator, and the next the room started spinning, and the person in black came in, and then you shook me awake."

"A person in black came in?"

I nodded.

"Did you get a look at them?"

"No, I...not really. It's all kind of a blur. I heard screaming, maybe arguing." I paused. "Definitely arguing, and someone crying—a woman, I think—oh, did you get the paper? What did it say?"

"What do you mean, paper?"

"I mean, like a letter or something. It fell to the ground, but that's all I remember. It just kind of appeared and fell." I rubbed my temples again. My head really hurt. "It was all blurry and foggy, and a white smoky haze filled the room."

His eyes fixed on mine, and he held up two fingers. "How many fingers do you see?"

"Four, five counting your thumb."

"Really?"

"Do you want to know how many you held up? If so, it was two."

"Austin told me you fell down the stairs at work the other day. Maybe you have a concussion. You need to see Doc."

"I'm fine," I said, my voice stern and determined. "I don't have a concussion." My legs ached, but that usually happened when I went through something intense. My body responded to stress in unusual ways. I breathed in deeply letting the air fill my lungs and sat a moment before releasing it. "Did the cooks see anything? Did they see the person dressed in black?"

"I've got a deputy questioning them now."

"Okay."

"Chantilly, go to Doc Bramblett. Have him take a look at you. I'll come by and check on you in a bit and get an official statement."

I grumbled and moaned, not wanting to see the doctor but realizing my behavior bordered on childish and stubborn. Strange things had been happening ever since I fell, I had to admit that. I also had to admit, at least to myself, that it was entirely possible I'd jarred my brain in some way to cause those strange things to happen.

Seeing shadows, hearing voices, and watching tails of

wedding dress trains scoot across the floor attached to nothing wasn't normal, so I had to have knocked my noggin up good.

"Chantilly?" Jack caught my attention when he waved his hand in front of my face.

"Yes?"

"You didn't hear a word I said, did you?"

"No, I didn't. I'm sorry. I was thinking about something."

He pushed his eyebrows together and pursed his lips. "Are you okay? I can get the paramedic to take you to the hospital."

I shook my head. "No, no. It's okay. I'm fine. I can get to Doc's on my own."

"Okay. I'll come by in a bit, okay?"

"Sure." I strolled off still a bit dazed and confused. At the end of the restaurant's driveway, I turned around and gazed at the building and there, in the window of Bobby's office, was Agnes Hamilton waving directly at me.

CHAPTER 3

*D*oc Bramblett was old school when it came to medicine. His office took up the front half of his home, and he still made house calls. Half the town didn't have health insurance, or couldn't afford to pay him, but that didn't matter to Doc. He'd gathered an impressive, if not unique, collection of valuables in lieu of payment, and was proud to show them off. The three deer heads hanging in his reception area were payment from the Jackson family. They'd offered two more, but Mrs. Doc, as she'd been nicknamed during my childhood, put a stop to that. She preferred fresh eggs, homemade bacon, chocolate chip cookies, and pies over dead animals.

I understood where she was coming from. If I had my choice, I'd choose chocolate chip cookies over the intimidating stare of a dead animal's eyes every day.

Doc saw me right away, and gave me a serious what-for for not coming to him the day I'd unintentionally skipped the bottom half of the stairs. "You could have internal bleeding or swelling dear. You got to take better care of yourself."

Ouch, a verbal switch to the heart, that's what that was. "I don't think it's that serious."

He poked and prodded the bump. "Does it hurt?"

"Only when you touch it."

He laughed. "Have you thrown up since you fell?"

"No, sir."

"Eating okay?"

"Yes, sir."

"Did you lose consciousness? He sat in front of me and pressed into my temples. "Does that hurt?"

I pulled away. "Ouch. And yes, Olivia said I was out for a few seconds, but I don't recall. I think it probably jarred me and that's it. I did pass out at Hamilton House a little bit ago, but I'm assuming that was situational, not because of my head."

"What happened at Hamilton House?"

I told him about Bobby Pruitt and how I'd discovered him, got dizzy and passed out.

"Oh, heavens, that's awful. Who would do a thing like that?"

"It was awful, and I have no idea. It was shocking to see him like that, which is why I think I passed out."

"Well, at least he's with his momma now. Boy never was the same without her."

Bobby wasn't the nicest guy in town, and if that had a part in where his soul rested, I worried for the guy.

He pulled my upper eyelids up and flashed his little light into my eyes. "Most people that lose consciousness don't realize it's happened. I'm inclined to trust Olivia on this." He checked my ears. "Any ringing or buzzing?"

"Whispers and a bit of laughing, but that's about it."

He pushed his rolling chair directly in front of me. "Excuse me?"

My shoulders slumped. "And I've seen a few strange things, too."

He rolled his chair back and opened the manila folder on his small cart. "You're hearing whispers and laughing? Do you feel paranoid? Like people are talking about you?"

I laughed. "No, not like that. I mean actual whispers and laughing, but there's no one there." I knew that sounded like I'd lost my mind, but I wanted to be honest. "I'm sure it was my imagination."

The wrinkles around the older man's eyes deepened. "Seeing stars?"

"No, not stars exactly. More like shadows and things."

He scratched at his temple. "You're seeing things now?"

I sighed. "I'm not making sense, am I? I'm not seeing things, and I'm not hearing things exactly." I shook my head. "Maybe I am. I don't know. I don't know how to explain it. I just feel a little off, so I'm probably making things seem worse than they really are."

I didn't expand on my situation because I feared giving him the specifics would make me sound even worse than he'd thought.

Doc tapped my knee with a tiny hammer-like instrument, and the bottom of my leg jerked forward. "You definitely have a concussion. I don't think it's a bad one, but I think we need to get you some tests over at the hospital just in case."

"Is that really necessary?"

He made a soft humming sound. "It's not every day a patient of mine comes in talking about hearing people and seeing shadows, Chantilly. If your mother were here, she'd want you to go, too. Lord knows that old woman would have driven you there herself."

My mother would have, the old stubborn biddy she was. I sure missed her something awful. "Can I give it a few days, maybe see if things improve? I've had a lot happening in my life lately, Doc. I'm sure it's just stress."

He narrowed his eyes at me, and I knew he was thinking about it. "Okay, here's what we'll do. I want you to go home, take it easy, ice that bump on your head, though it's probably a little too late for that, and then come back and see me next week. If you're still having issues, it's off to the hospital you go, you hear me?"

"Loud and clear, Doc. Loud and clear."

———

I called Olivia on my way home from Doc's office. "I'm sorry I haven't checked in."

"Oh, sweetie, bless your heart. I heard what happened. Are you okay? I've been so worried. Where have you been? I called you twice but you didn't answer. Oh, and that poor Bobby Pruitt, God rest his soul. Terrible. It's just terrible."

"I know, and I'm fine. I went to Doc's. I figured I'd better go and get checked."

"Oh, thank heavens. What did he say?"

"He thinks it's a concussion and wants me to get some rest, so I'm heading home for the rest of the day."

"Well, of course you are. Even without a concussion—which I knew you had, by the way—you should go home and rest. After the morning you've had, you need it. How about I bring over some lunch later? I can pick something up from Del's place."

"That's not necessary. I'm don't think I could eat anything anyway, but thank you."

"It's nothing."

I dragged myself to my bedroom and changed into my comfy clothes while Cooper stretched out on the bed and watched. Fully intending to stay home the rest of the day, I scrubbed my face clean of makeup, applied my strongest moisturizer, and shuffled to the kitchen.

I stepped past the downstairs bathroom and stopped when I heard the familiar deep voice from inside.

"Baby girl."

I backed up and glanced into the bathroom. "Daddy?" I shook my head. "What am I thinking?" I knew the stories of people that thought they heard the voices of their dead loved ones but that sounded so real. I stood in the hallway and stared up at the ceiling. "Daddy? Are you here?"

No one whispered back, and my heart sank. I missed my dad something fierce. I pulled my hands into the sleeves of my extra large Auburn sweatshirt and shivered as a chill rushed through me.

I poured myself a tall glass of iced tea and snuggled up under a fuzzy blanket that had been in the house since high school as I watched daytime talk shows in the den.

The chilly air filling the house concerned me. My phone's weather app said it was ninety-six degrees outside, and the thermostat said it was seventy-three in the house. So, why was I cold? I kicked the temperature up to seventy-five and thought I'd have to call someone out next week to check it.

"Baby girl."

I opened my eyes. "Daddy, is that you?"

He smiled down at me. "Of course it's me. You've got a big responsibility now, but you can handle it. I know you'll make me and your momma proud."

I stared up at him and blinked. "I don't understand. What responsibility?"

He brushed my cheek with his hand. The rough edges of his fingertips felt familiar, like home. "Not just her. There will be others."

And then a group of people laughed loudly as I danced to Michael Jackson in a country bar.

I opened my eyes. The audience on the talk show was laughing and applauding. I blinked and scanned the room, hoping with all of my heart I'd see my daddy standing in the doorway, smiling at me like he always did.

But I didn't. I knew it was a dream, but it felt so real, the touch of his fingers, the air in the room, everything. I closed my eyes again, begging and praying I'd go back to that same dream, but I didn't. I couldn't sleep at all.

I practically jumped off the couch when someone knocked on my door. I stretched as I stood, not realizing how exhausted I was. I snuck a quick peek out the window, and Jack smiled at me. I checked the time on my phone. Austin was at lacrosse practice, so I assumed the assistant coach was handling it.

"Hey, come on in."

His smile didn't falter. "You go see Doc?"

I nodded as I padded toward the kitchen. "Minor concussion, nothing big. Would you like something to drink?"

"I'm good, but thanks."

I swapped my iced tea for a coffee. "I take it you're not going to make it to lacrosse practice?"

He shook his head. "Duty calls."

"Do you have any leads?" I headed back to the den.

"We can talk about that."

I turned around and watched as he examined my home. "I haven't made any changes, other than bringing in some of mine and Austin's things. I've thought about it, but I just can't. Not yet."

He nodded. "My dad's kept his house the same as it was the day my mom died. Said it feels like she's still there."

I understood. "Didn't your mom pass in the nineties?"

"Eighty-nine. Still has the green appliances. Did get himself a new microwave though." He scratched his chin. "Actually, I think he's had a few, but I'm not sure."

"Well, that's something."

"He had to get the first new one. Tried to cook a TV dinner in a microwave tray and melted the plastic in the oven."

I laughed. "Daddy probably would have done the same thing."

"I know I said it before, but I'm really sorry about your

parents. They were good people. I used to have coffee at the park with your dad every now and again."

I hoped that one day people sharing their memories of my parents wouldn't feel like knives stabbing straight into my heart, but that day must have been miles away because I couldn't even fathom it. "Thank you."

We sat in the den. Jack rubbed his hands together. "I'd like to get your statement, and when you're feeling better, I thought we could take a trip over to Hamilton House. I'm hoping you'll walk me through what happened."

I jumped from the couch. "Can we go now?"

"Uh, shouldn't you be resting?"

"I tried to sleep, but something woke me up, and I'd rather just get it over with. I'm not sure I'll ever go there again otherwise."

"Sure." He eyed my thick socks, baggy pajama bottoms, and big sweatshirt. "But you might be a little hot in that."

I glanced down at my clothing. "Oh, yes. Let me change right quick."

His lips curved into a smile.

Five minutes later we were in his car and headed to the restaurant.

"Is this your personal car?"

He nodded. "I have a department issued one, but I like to use my own when I'm dealing with witnesses. I hate making them sit in the back."

"And we thank you for that. I imagine that would be quite intimidating."

"That's not always a bad thing." His cell phone beeped, but he ignored it.

Yellow crime scene tape blocked the entrance to Hamilton House. As I stepped out of Jack's car, I checked Bobby's office window for a glimpse of Agnes Hamilton, but she wasn't there. I closed the car door and stood there, staring at the building. I chewed on my nail, but when I realized what I was doing, yanked it out of my mouth.

"It's okay to be nervous. Most people would be. Just take your time. When you're ready, we'll go in."

I took a deep breath. "I'm fine," I lied.

He smiled. "Okay, so what happened?" We walked to the entrance, and Jack opened the door and held the yellow tape up for me to step under. "Start from when you walked in." He closed the door behind me.

A chill rushed over me, and I rubbed my arms. I took a moment to focus, my eyes darting around the open space and up at the ceiling. A flash of white swung from a rope and then disappeared. I trembled.

Jack touched my arm, and I jerked forward.

"It's okay, Chantilly. We don't have to do this. I can take you home and get your statement there."

I shook my head. "No, no. It's okay. I'm sorry. I'm just a little nervous, but I'll be fine." I checked the rafter again, but my imagination must have gotten the best of me because there wasn't a thing there.

I explained how I'd arrived, walked into the kitchen, and asked to see Bobby. We retraced my steps and headed up to the offices. I let my fingers trail along the banister as I climbed, wondering how many times Agnes Hamilton had done that very same thing.

Bobby's office was located at the back end of the hall, and when we got to it, I froze. "I'm sorry. This is harder than I thought it would be."

He nodded. "Take your time."

I breathed in and blew the breath out as I straightened my shoulders. "I'm fine."

He opened the door, and I suddenly lost my balance. I stumbled back and hit the wall. I squeezed my eyes shut as the room began to spin, but it didn't help. It was happening all over again.

A white cloud.

A person dressed in black.

A rope.

A knife.

A letter dropping to the ground.

A deep guttural scream.

And then darkness.

"Chantilly? Chantilly? Wake up."

I opened my eyes. "What? What happened?"

Jack's face was millimeters from mine. "You fainted."

I pushed myself upright. "Again?"

"Again." He helped me the rest of the way up. "This was a bad idea. I'm sorry."

I held up my hand. "No, it's okay. I want to do this. I need to." I went over what happened when I discovered Bobby dead in his chair. Seeing him crumpled over in a heap at his desk. The white cloud, the person in black, the knife, the letter, all of it.

"We never found the letter."

"Maybe it wasn't a letter. Maybe it was just a piece of paper." I pressed my fingertips into my temples. "It feels like it was a letter though. I don't understand. How could you not find a piece of paper?"

I scanned Bobby's office and there were papers in piles all over his desk. "Great. It could be any one of those." I ran my hand through my brown hair. "Did the cooks see the person in black? He, or she, I guess, could have gone unnoticed, but did you ask?"

He nodded. "They didn't see anyone but you."

"Did you talk to Maybelle? I saw her on my way here. She was really upset."

"Upset? Why? The cooks told us she was off. I was planning to talk to her today."

"You should. She didn't take the day off. Bobby fired her. That's what she was upset about."

"He fired her? When?"

"She made it sound like it had just happened."

"Did she say why?"

"He'd found out she entered the barbecue competition."

He nodded. "Sounds like Bobby." He walked behind the desk and picked up a paper. He quickly read it, put it down, and picked up another one, and did the same thing until he'd finished several of them. "There's nothing here but bills, statements, inventory lists. You don't have any idea what the paper had on it?"

"I really can't even be sure I saw a paper. It's all so blurry. It's almost like I dreamed it all in slow motion or something." I pressed my fingertips into the lower part of my skull under my ears. "I don't understand."

He smiled. "It's okay. We'll figure it out." He guided me out the door, and as he closed it behind him, a shadow appeared inside the office.

I gasped. "Wait. Open the door. I think someone's in there."

He stood there for a second, just staring at me like I'd lost my mind. "No one's there, Chantilly."

I clenched my fists and shook them at my sides. "Please, just open it. I'm sure I saw something."

He turned the handle and pushed the door open.

I pressed my shoulders back and marched in there ready to prove to Jack Levitt how right I was. Only, there wasn't anyone inside the room. Not a single soul.

Jack meandered over to a window, took a look outside then moved on to the other two. "It's windy out today." He pointed to a large maple tree in the back yard of the restaurant. "Probably saw a shadow from this."

I checked out the window, but I knew it wasn't the shadow of a tree. I just didn't have a clue what it was. "Yeah, I guess," I lied. What was I supposed to say? Jack already thought I was crazy.

"They say Agnes likes to mess with people. Maybe she's messing with you."

He laughed, but I didn't think it was all that funny. Instead, I thought he was onto something. I wouldn't say I believed in ghosts, but since my parents passed, I wanted to believe in the possibility. Of course, I didn't want to believe spirits were grounded to the earth because of something negative. I preferred to believe that if they were still with us, it was because they chose to be. "May I have a moment?"

"In here?"

I nodded. "Please? It might help me remember something. I just feel like I need to be here. Alone." The feeling overwhelmed me, actually, but I didn't want him to question my emotional state. I'd already appeared a bit on the crazy side.

He walked back to the door. "Take your time."

After he closed the door, I sat in the chair in front of Bobby's desk and waited. For what, I wasn't sure, but I just knew something would happen. I felt it in my bones.

I tried to relax. I loosened my shoulders, dropped my arms over the sides of the chair, and shook my hands. I breathed in and out like I'd learned in yoga class, but nothing helped, so I just waited. When the hairs on my arms lifted, and goosebumps spread across them, and a swift burst of cold air surrounded me, I gripped the chair's arms and held my breath, white knuckled and nervous.

Breathe, Chantilly. Just breathe.

A small warm breath of air touched my left ear, and the hairs on the back of my neck stiffened. "It was him," a woman's voice whispered.

I jerked in my seat. "Hello?" Shifting my head from side to side, I tried to stay calm, but it wasn't easy. "Who are you? Agnes? Is that you? Who? Who was him? What does that even mean?" My lips quivered as I spoke. I was afraid, very afraid.

The chill in the room deepened even more, and even though every muscle in my body was tight and tense, I shook uncontrollably. Beads of sweat formed on my temples, but I didn't dare move to wipe them. It took all of the strength I had to stay in that seat and not bolt out the door. "Is someone here with me? Please, do something. Say something." I squeezed my eyes shut and licked my lips.

A flash of cold air rushed past me, and I jumped out of my seat when a large binder flew off the desk and hit the wall behind me.

The door burst open. "What's going on?" Jack rushed in and charged toward me. "What happened?"

My mouth hung open, but I couldn't form the words. "I…uh, I…" I pointed to the binder lying on the floor. "That."

He picked it up and placed it on the desk. "It's a binder."

I shook my head. "No, you don't understand. It…I…It—" I swung my finger back and forth, pointing to where the binder was and where it ended up, all the while babbling like a toddler trying to find her words.

"Breathe, Chantilly." His reassuring smile chipped away at my panic, and my heart rate dropped back to an almost normal speed.

I took a deep breath and blew it out slowly. "It just…I don't know. It just flew across the room and into the wall. Out of nowhere. I…I didn't even touch it. I was sitting in the chair."

He raised an eyebrow. "The binder just picked itself up and sailed across the room? On its own?"

It didn't sound logical, but it happened. I saw it with my own eyes. "Yes, out of nowhere, it just flew across the room."

He pinched the bridge of his nose. "You have a concussion. I shouldn't have brought you here. It's too much stress. You need to be resting." He took me by the arm and led me out of the room.

I looked back in that short distance and saw a white cloud float down into the floor and disappear.

We didn't say much as we drove back to my house. Jack asked me if I needed to see Doc Bramblett, but I shook my head. "I'm fine, but thank you." I sat quietly for another moment, but I couldn't take it anymore, and I had to say something. "I know you don't believe me, but the binder really did fly across the room."

He glanced at me, but only for a moment, and then his eyes went straight back to the road. "I don't not believe you, Chantilly. I just don't know how a binder can fling itself across a room like that."

It didn't fling itself. Someone flung it. "What if it was Agnes Hamilton?"

He blinked and shook his head. "A ghost? You think a ghost picked up the binder and tossed it at you? Come on, that's kind of out there, don't you think?"

"I don't think she was trying to hit me."

"Agnes Hamilton is long dead. Even if I did believe her ghost was hanging around Hamilton House, I'd be hard pressed to believe she threw a binder across the room."

"I would have said the same thing, but now I'm not so sure."

We arrived at my house, and Jack turned off the car and held onto the steering wheel for a moment before getting out. He walked me to my door. "Can you call someone? Have them sit with you until Austin's home? I'm not sure you should be alone."

"I'm fine, I promise. I have to get him in a bit anyway."

"No, you shouldn't be driving. I really think you need to go to see Doc. He could run some tests or something. I think the concussion is worse than he thought."

I probably wouldn't have believed me either, but it didn't matter. I knew what happened was real.

I just didn't know what it meant.

Jack refused to let me pick up Austin from practice, and after ten minutes of attempting to convince him I was fine, I finally gave in and let him drive me to the field.

Jack talked with the team and the assistant coach while I walked around the small track that outlined the playing fields. I worked to mentally piece together the puzzle of situations I'd recently experienced. Was that Agnes Hamilton? Did she whisper in my ear? And what did it's him mean? Was she referring to Bobby? She couldn't have been, could she? Was she trying to give me a message about him? Did he kill himself like she'd done? He'd have to have been pretty darn flexible to do that, and though I hadn't spent much time with Bobby Pruitt ever, I would bet my lifesavings the man wasn't flexible enough to contort that way.

What did it all mean then? The knife. The letter. Yes, the letter. I was certain I'd seen a piece of paper drop to the ground, yet Jack said there wasn't one. Everything was blurry and hazy, but something inside me told me it was a letter, not just a piece of paper. A letter the police didn't find anywhere in the office.

What did it all mean?

I caught up to Jack and Austin on the way to the car, and Austin didn't even flinch when we got to Jack's and not mine. He acted like it was the most natural thing to do. I wished I had his bounceback ability, or naïvety, whichever it was. "Can we stop for food? I'm starving."

Jack wrapped his arm around Austin's shoulders. "Sure, buddy, I could use a bite, too. How's pizza sound?"

I grimaced. "It's a school night, and besides, you really want to take this kid out in public with the way he smells?"

Austin sniffed his armpits, and I gagged just at the thought of that. "I smell fine."

Jack laughed. "I wouldn't go that far, but I don't think you'll clear out a pizza joint."

"I wouldn't put it past him, and besides, I'm sure you've got homework, right, Austin?"

"Come on, Mom, it's just one night. I can get my homework done when I get home."

"Yeah, it's just one night, Mom," Jack said, a smile stretched across his face. "I think I've got some air freshener in my trunk. I can spray it on him, and he'll be good as new."

Austin's words echoed his lacrosse coach's. "Yeah, good as new."

I sighed. The fact that earlier Jack thought I'd needed to go home and rest didn't even come up, but at least he'd stopped suggesting I go back to see Doc Bramblett. "Fine, but no dilly dallying. We eat and we leave. That's it. You hear me?"

Jack saluted me, and Austin copied him, and I knew then he had a fan, and I'd never win an argument when he was around again. His phone rang as we parked in the lot of Pizzaso's Pizza Parlor. He checked the screen and silenced it.

"If you need to get that, we can get a table."

"It's not important."

I wondered if the person on the other end of the line agreed.

We ordered our pizza and Austin filled us in on practice.

"Then Coach Tom had us running sprints." He slurped his soda up through the straw. "At the end of practice. How stupid is that?"

"Austin, don't call your coach stupid. That's disrespectful," I said.

"Well, it was."

Jack smirked. "I get it. You're tired, and the last thing you wanted to do was run, but there's a method to that madness."

"Like what, torture?" Austin asked.

"Exactly," Jack said. "It's our goal to send you home exhausted and beaten down so you don't give your momma a hard time."

I laughed. "I appreciate the effort, but I don't think it's working."

"Nana says I'm an angel." Austin frowned. "Well, that's what she used to say."

I covered the top of his hand with mine, and with a serious tone, said, "That's because she didn't live with you."

Jack laughed. "He's a pretty good kid most of the time."

"It's the rest of the time that's an issue." I smiled at my son. "But he's cute, and he says please and thank you, so I'll keep him."

Austin smiled. "Does that mean I can have ice cream for dessert?"

Jack and I both said no at the same time. When he smiled at me, I blushed.

His phone rang again. I snuck a peek at it lying on the table. It was Lonna. He silenced it again.

"You should get that, really."

He stared into my eyes then at his phone. He picked it up, said, excuse me, and walked away from the table.

Austin stuck his head into his phone, and I went back to thinking about what happened earlier in Bobby's office.

CHAPTER 4

*D*el set the coffee pot down on the counter. "The binder flew off the desk all by itself?"

I checked behind me and whispered. "You don't have to announce it to the world."

She poured half and half into my coffee, slid the cup to me, and then crooked her finger as she walked from behind the counter. I followed her to the corner table in the backside of the café.

"Had to be Agnes. She's been known to do that kind of thing."

"Do you really believe in ghosts, Del?" I sipped my coffee and waited while she finished drinking hers. Given the way things had gone, I'd changed my tune on ghosts. I preferred that theory to internal bleeding or some kind of brain damage from my concussion. Believing in ghosts was a whole lot easier when crazy things happened. Crazy things like whispers and binders flying across rooms.

Jack walked through the door before she had a chance to answer. Delphina eyed him with a lusty look. "Hmm, hmm, talk about improving with age. That man is like a nice bottle of wine that's been sitting in my basement for years."

I told her to hush as he approached us. "Ew, that's creepy, and besides, he can hear you."

"You think I'm worried about that?"

No, I didn't. Not one bit.

"Ladies." He nodded and smiled at me. "Thanks again for dinner last night. You really didn't have to do that."

"Dinner?" Del raised her eyebrow, but I ignored it.

"You shouldn't have paid for me and my son," I said, stressing the me and my son part.

"A gentleman never lets a woman pay on a date," Del said.

"Well, it wasn't a date, so he should have let me pay."

She leaned back in her chair and crossed her arms over her chest. "Emm, hmm. When a man and a woman go out to eat, it's always a date."

"We picked up Austin at practice, and he was hungry. It wasn't a date."

Jack chuckled but didn't offer me any support.

"And why were the two of you together in the first place?"

"I told you already. We went back to Hamilton House to walk through what happened, remember?"

"Chantilly's got a minor concussion, and I didn't want her driving, so I offered to pick up Austin, and he was hungry, so we went and grabbed a bite at Pizzaso's."

Del gave him a once over. "That was mighty thoughtful of you, Detective. Tell me, how's Lonna feel about you going out to dinner with another woman?" She winked at him.

I blushed. "Delphina, don't you be making trouble where there isn't any." I sat there gritting my teeth and trying not to make things worse. Lonna and I had a history, one that wasn't all that pretty, and I didn't want to add fuel to that fire. Lord knew I already had enough going on.

"Let me get your coffee, sweetie. You just have a seat. I'll only be a minute." She stood and sauntered back to the counter as if Jack had all the time in the world.

"I'm sorry about that," I said, my face still burning with embarrassment.

"Don't be. Del's been trying to marry me off for years. I'm used to it."

"You're dating Lonna now, so maybe Del can focus her efforts on planning your wedding."

He blinked. "Wedding? What? No, it's not that serious. It's not serious at all, actually. I'm not ready for that. Heck, I'm not ready to use the word dating. It's a lot of effort to be in a relationship and drilling it down to one word like that makes me nervous."

"I can relate to that. But Lonna, I sure hope she knows how you feel."

He changed the subject. "How're you feeling?"

"I'm fine, thank you. Really, I don't know what happened yesterday. I'm sure the binder just fell and then slid across the floor or something. I'm sure I overreacted."

He didn't argue. "Probably."

"Never mind the big rug on the floor."

"You heading over to Doc Bramblett's again?"

Del handed him a large to-go cup and saved me from giving him an excuse. "Here ya go, sugar. Just how you like it."

He handed her a five dollar bill but she refused to take it. "Men in uniform get free coffee here, and you know that."

"It's a tip, Delphina, and a well deserved one."

She smiled. "Well then, how can I refuse?" She snatched the bill right out of his hands.

He laughed, and I liked the way it sounded. Bold and strong, but not too loud, and genuine. Scott never laughed from the heart. His laugh always had a twinge of sarcasm attached to it.

"Hmm, hmm. I'll say it again. That man is a mighty fine lookin' man." Del sat in the chair across from me, eying Jack's back side and nodding as he left the café. "All that goodness packed into muscle and tight pants, why a woman could get lost in all that manliness."

"Yes, I'm sure Lonna's lost in it every day."

She lifted the right side of her mouth. "Sugar, that woman don't know what to do with a man like that."

"And you do?"

"'Course I do, and I can teach you, too." She smiled. "But I ain't sure you could handle it."

"I am not interested, but thank you."

"It doesn't matter if you're interested. That man is, that much I know. Did you see the way he looked at you? Men don't look at women like that unless they're picturing them naked."

A flush crept up my neck and brightened my cheeks. "Delphina, stop it. That's crazy talk, and you know it. He's worried about my head, about what I saw last night. He thinks I'm crazy. He is not interested in me."

"You keep thinking that honey, but I know men, and that man has got the hots for you."

"Can we please get back to the…" I paused and then whispered, "you know, Agnes situation?"

"I know how we can solve it right quick. Just say the word."

"The word."

It took a second for that to sink in. "We have ourselves a little séance, that's how."

I laughed. "You can't be serious. Nobody does that for real."

"Of course they do. Unless you've got yourself a psychic power it's the only way to communicate with them. Well, that and those Ouija boards, but I won't mess with those things." She leaned toward me. "I hear they're evil."

"Bless your heart, you're just as crazy as Jack thinks I am."

"I may be, but I'm the crazy woman that's offering you a solution."

She made a lot of sense, at least about that part. "I wouldn't even know how to perform a séance."

She waved that off with a flick of her hand. "Don't you worry about that. I've seen 'em a hundred times on TV. I watch a lot of those haunting shows. I'm an old pro. Plus, you can find anything on the internet these days."

"How much time do you spend on the internet?"

Thelma and Olivia walked in together, waving at us from the door.

"Hey, y'all. Is this the girls' club?" Olivia asked.

"With her here, it's more like the toddlers' club," Del said.

I jabbed her hand with my pointer finger. "Be nice."

She grunted.

Thelma dragged her favorite chair from across the room. I laughed as Del's jaw stiffened. She did an excellent job not giving Thelma a verbal lashing, though. I was impressed.

"I'll take my regular," Thelma said. "And this time, please put the right amount of sugar in it. Last time you cheated me a packet." She wiggled her finger at Del. "Don't think I couldn't tell."

"Don't think I couldn't tell," Del muttered as she walked to the counter. "You keep being so high maintenance, I'll tell you where you can stick that packet."

"It's supposed to go in my coffee," Thelma hollered.

"That ain't where I'm talking about," Delphina hollered back.

Olivia and I stared at each other. "I'm afraid to order my drink," she said.

"The girl here wants her drink, too," Thelma yelled.

"Then she can come order it herself," Del shouted back.

"Excuse me," Olivia said. She walked to the counter, her shoulders slumped, and I suspected, fearing for her life.

Del lived for that kind of thing. Her favorite pastime was wearing her permanent bad mood on her shoulders, and she excelled at it.

I glanced at her as she prepared the drinks. An unfamiliar expression flashed on her face, but when she caught me watching, it disappeared.

"I saw that, Delphina Beauregard."

She refused to make eye contact.

"You're not fooling me."

"What did you see?" Thelma asked.

I adjusted myself back into my seat facing the table. "She smiled."

Thelma threw her hands in the air. "Sweet baby Jesus, it's a miracle."

"I heard that," Del yelled.

Thelma winked at me and chatted away. Olivia had returned and listened intently, but I hadn't heard a word. I excused myself for a moment and walked over to Del. "Sweetie, I'm sorry."

"It's okay, that woman has been yanking my chain for years now."

I moved around to her side of the counter. "No, I'm sorry about Bobby. I know you thought of him as family. I hadn't thought about how this would affect you, and I'm sorry for that, too." I hugged her, and she hugged me back.

"Bobby wasn't the most popular man in town. I'm surprised it took this long for something to happen."

"You don't really feel that way."

She nodded. "He was kin to me, and I loved his momma like the dickens, but that boy, no matter what anyone said or did, he had a fireball of anger inside of him, and nothing nobody could do could put it out. When you live like that, you're bound to die in a pit of flames." She gave me a soft smile. "He's with his momma now, the Lord willin', and I'm happy for that." She handed me Olivia's drink. "Help me get these to them, will ya?"

I obliged.

"I can't believe what's happened," Olivia said.

Thelma shook her head. "Don't know who could have done something so terrible."

"I bet there's a long list," Del said.

Thelma gasped. "Delphina Beauregard, do not speak ill of the dead."

"I'm not saying anything I wouldn't have said to Bobby's face, and he knows it."

Olivia and I made eye contact. She went to speak, but I shook my head. Better safe than sorry, I thought.

Del's face lit up, and her eyes widened. "But you know what? There's a way to find out who did this to Bobby. I was just telling Chantilly here about it."

"I don't think we should talk about—"

Olivia leaned in, curiosity spreading across her face. "What's that?"

"A séance, that's how."

Thelma coughed. "Those things where you call for the dead to come?" She shook her head. "I don't know. My cousin did one of those once and his house burned to the ground." She sipped her drink. "Firemen came and said it was the cat knocking over a candle, but he ran off and never came back, so we'll never know."

"Every time you open your mouth something crazy comes out," Del said.

"Takes one to know one," Thelma said.

"Miss Thelma," Olivia whispered. "That doesn't make sense."

Del shook her head. "See what I mean?"

"Goodness, you two are going to be the death of me. I really need to make friends my own age," I said.

Del jabbed me on the arm. "I bet Lonna's going to have some free time soon."

"Hush."

She laughed. "I'm serious about the séance. I think we all go over to Hamilton House and see if we can get Bobby or Agnes to chat with us. They might could give us a hinkerin' about what happened."

Olivia rubbed her hands together. "Oh, that sounds like fun. My favorite movie is Casper. I've always wanted to see a ghost."

Del rolled her eyes. "That's a cartoon character."

"In the movie he was computerized," Olivia said.

I stared into my almost empty cup. "I'm not sure this is a good idea."

"It's awfully dangerous," Thelma said.

"What bad can come from Hamilton House?" Del asked.

"Bobby Joe Pruitt wasn't a nice man. I bet he's not a nice ghost, either."

"Don't you worry about him. I can handle Bobby just fine."

Olivia chimed in. "I've read ghosts are only mean when something bad's happened."

We all stared at her.

"Oh, well, I didn't think that through before I said it, did I?"

"Wouldn't be the first time," Del said.

"Delphina, be nice," I said.

"I've seen a bunch of them on the TV. They don't seem all that hard, but no cats." Thelma shook her head. "Definitely no cats."

I raised both of my eyebrows at Delphina.

"At least we agree on something," she said.

"What exactly did you find agreeable in that?" I asked.

"We both watch them on TV. We know what to do."

"I'm not sure I—"

Del cut Thelma off. "I know what to do."

"Miss Delphina, when did you want to do this?" Olivia asked. "Aren't they supposed to be done at night?"

"That's usually how it works."

"I go to bed at nine-thirty. I need me my beauty sleep," Thelma said.

"It ain't helpin'," Del said.

Thelma patted her face and then pulled her compact out of her purse. "Oh dear, she might be right."

"I don't want to be out too late. I don't like leaving Austin home alone at night."

"It's best we do it tonight or the day after tomorrow. I don't wash my hair on these nights," Olivia said.

"All y'all need to get out more." Del huffed loudly. "Tonight it is. We'll meet here at eight o'clock. That'll give everyone enough time for their beauty treatments before they turn back to pumpkins." She smiled at me. "And maybe that new friend of yours can watch over your son for a bit."

———

I packed a bag of candles from the kitchen and tossed in two matchbooks from the drawer in the pantry. Momma always grabbed matchbooks whenever we went out, and she'd leave them in a bowl in the front hall. I couldn't bear to toss them, so I stuffed them in a drawer in the kitchen pantry. As I packed the bag, I told Austin I had a meeting, which wasn't exactly a lie.

"Why're you bringing candles?"

"Oh, Delphina asked me to loan her some." I hated lying, and I wasn't very good at it. Who returned burned candles? "Bed time is ten o'clock, and I mean it." I shut off the overhead kitchen light. "No video games until your homework is done either, okay?"

"I know the rules, Momma. I'm not a child."

"Says who?"

"Says everyone my age."

"And there you go." I kissed his cheek. "Behave, you old man. Love you."

"Love you too, old lady."

Ouch.

I wasn't the last to arrive at Community Café. Thelma showed up five minutes after me in her pajamas and robe.

Del tilted her head almost ninety degrees when she saw her. "What in the devil are you doing out like that?"

"Like what?"

She waved her hand up and down. "Like you got out of bed and drove straight here."

"I thought we'd be out late, and I didn't want to have to get ready for bed so late, so I decided to do it before I got here."

Del just stood there, unable to respond.

Olivia raised her hand "Excuse me, but how exactly are we supposed to get into Hamilton House?"

From the look on Del's face, I knew it was going to be a long night, at least for her. "I got a key, that's how," she said.

"Oh."

"I brought candles. I figured we'd need them, but I'd like to say one more time I don't think this is smart. We could be getting in over our heads."

Olivia slumped into a chair inside the café. "I agree. We could hire a professional. You know, one of those psychics from the county fair?"

"We don't need one of them. I know what I'm doing. Y'all just got to trust me."

I stood and stretched. I hadn't realized I was so tired.

"You sure you're okay to be doing this?" Olivia asked. "You have a concussion, maybe you should go home and get some rest."

"I'm fine, really. I'm not sure why I even decided this was a good idea, but we're all here, so let's just go and get it over with."

Del locked the door behind us.

Olivia grabbed my arm as we walked over to Hamilton House. "We can't get in trouble for this, can we? My daddy will have a heart attack if I get arrested. Our good name will be ruined."

"We won't get arrested," Del said.

Thelma tightened the belt of her robe. "I sure hope not. I would look horrible in my mugshot with my hair like this."

Even though I couldn't see her, I knew with one hundred percent confidence that Delphina just rolled her eyes. Del unlocked the back door to the kitchen and let us all in before she walked in and locked it behind her.

"It's different here," Thelma said.

"It sure is," Olivia said.

"What'd you expect? Bobby's dead. It won't ever be the same."

Thelma whispered, "I'm going to miss the way he always acted so cranky."

Del stopped. "That wasn't an act."

We crept into the main dining area, guided of course, by Del's flashlight. I peered up at the ceiling rafters, but thankfully, I didn't see anything. Everyone else looked up there too.

"Hard as I've tried, I've never seen Agnes Hamilton or none of the ghosts said to be haunting Castleberry," Thelma said.

Olivia stared up at the rafters again. "I saw the spirit at the cemetery when I was a teenager. The one in the long white dress with the crazy hair. What's her name again?"

"America Hall," both Thelma and Delphina said.

"Yes, America Hall. A lovely name."

I'd forgotten about America Hall's story. The history in Castleberry was rich, like most old towns, especially the ones in the South. The Civil War took its toll on Georgia, but if anything, it left us with a deeper commitment to our roots, and a whole lot of ghost stories to tell on Christmas.

Why we did that, I had no idea, but it was tradition.

America Hall was pregnant during the last part of the War, and miscarried when she got the news that her husband had died in battle. The pain and shock over losing both her husband and her child sent her over the edge, and understandably so. One morning townspeople found her lying on her husband's grave, like she'd fallen asleep and then just died. In fact, at first they thought she was sleeping, but when they touched her to wake her, she was cold. They said she died of a broken heart, and since then, her spirit's been haunting the cemetery, looking for her husband and child.

As a child I always wondered if she'd ever find them, but I suspected she hadn't.

"This ought to work." Delphina set her bag on a table in the center part of the dining room. "Chantilly, on second thought, spread your candles out in a circle about three quarters out, but not too close to the edge. We need some room."

Thelma moved around the room. "There aren't any cats in here, are there?"

"It's a restaurant, Thelma," Del said. She lit some incense and waved at the small stream of smoke as it floated from the thin stick.

Thelma pinched her nose with her fingers. "Pee ew. That smells horrible."

"It ain't supposed to smell good to us. It's supposed to attract spirits."

"Smells like it's gonna attract something all right. Something like a cat. Or maybe a rat. Rats can knock down candles, too."

Olivia held her hand to her chest. "Oh, I'm afraid of rats. Their long skinny tails give me the willies."

"You and me both," I said.

Del shook her head and sighed. "Bless your ever loving hearts, you two are crazier than all get out. It's for the spirits. Spirits and rats don't like the same smells."

"Excuse me, but how exactly do you know that?" Olivia asked.

"I got connections."

Okay. Whatever that meant.

Del pulled out the chair in the center of the table. "Everyone take a seat. We've got to hold hands and recite a séance starting thingamajig."

Thelma pursed her lips. "What's a séance starting thingamajig?"

"Just pop a squat and repeat after me."

We all did as she said because when Delphina's tone bordered on terse, like it did then, we all knew we'd better listen. We feared what could happen otherwise.

"Now, let's hold hands, and everyone close your eyes."

I held on to Thelma and Del, but I would have preferred discussing the BBQ competition instead.

"We're calling on the light from above," Del said. She opened her left eye. I knew because I'd been watching her intently. "I said close your eyes."

I glanced at Olivia and Thelma, and their eyes were open, too.

"I had my eyes closed 'til you started talking," Thelma said.

"I'm sorry, Miss Delphina. I prefer to keep my eyes open. I'm not all that interested in surprises," Olivia said.

"You got to keep your eyes closed during the visitation request. That's the rules."

"Who wrote these rules?" Thelma asked.

Delphina growled, and I wasn't exaggerating.

"Ladies, I think there is a way of doing this, and Del's trying to follow it. She's researched this specifically for this evening, so it's probably best we do as she says." I hoped that would calm the battle before it started.

"Don't know why she's got to always be in charge," Thelma said.

"Because it was my idea," Del said.

"I have ideas, too."

Del stood, but I motioned for her to sit. "Y'all, I've got a son at home I'd like to get back to before sunrise, so how about we shelf the bickering until tomorrow? Besides, if Bobby's even considering coming by for a visit, he's not going to when everyone's got their undies in a bunch."

"I'm not wearing any undies," Thelma said. "These jammies got built-in liners. I got them at the Walmart down in Gainesville last week. They're comfy, too."

Del rolled her eyes again. She did that a lot around Thelma. "TMI, Thelma. TMI." She started her thingamajig to summon

Bobby Joe Pruitt's spirit again. "We're calling on the great and glorious light from above. We ask for your guidance and wish for your love to fill the room. We ask for only the spirit of Bobby Joe Pruitt, so may his soul forever rest in peace. Once we're done helping him do that, that is. We're here to help him get home. Bobby Joe Pruitt, are you here?"

A chill swept over me. I shivered. Thelma squeezed my hand tightly.

"Bobby Joe Pruitt, come to us," Del said.

Olivia coughed. "Excuse me."

The table trembled below our hands, and Thelma dug her fake nail tips into my palm.

"Did you feel that?" Olivia whispered.

I nodded. "It's okay. Happens all the time."

"All the time? Why, it's never happened to me. The only thing that shakes around me are my boobies, but I got a new bra, and it's made all the difference," Thelma said.

I chuckled and quickly pressed my lips together to stop myself. I stared up at the ceiling rafter, feeling the cold air fill my lungs as I breathed in. When I exhaled, I saw my breath.

Something was happening.

Olivia shivered. "It's awfully cold in here now. How low does Bobby keep the air conditioner?"

Delphina whispered, "It ain't the air conditioner, sweetie. It's Bobby."

She was definitely right. It wasn't the air conditioner, but it wasn't Bobby either.

It was Agnes Hamilton.

And I knew that because she was glowing right behind Delphina and staring directly at me.

CHAPTER 5

"*D*o you see that?" I asked. I pointed behind Delphina, shaking my finger at the cloudy image of a woman that had been dead for over a hundred years.

Delphina swiveled around. "See what?"

I jabbed my finger toward the spirit. "That. Agnes. She's right there, behind you."

Thelma squinted. "I don't see a thing."

"It's her concussion. She's been forgetting things, and now she's seeing things, too," Olivia said.

I turned toward her. "Olivia, I am not seeing things. She's right there." I pointed toward the spirit again. "How can you not see her?" I stared at the spirit, my mouth hanging open, and my eyes popped like I'd just gone down the big hill on a roller-coaster. Sure, I'd had fleeting moments, times when I thought I saw part of her dress, a time or two when I believed I'd seen Agnes herself, but they were nothing like the spirit standing behind Delphina's chair. If I hadn't known better, I would have thought we were in the middle of a movie production with a well-made up actress and excellent staging. But I did know better.

Del shrugged. "Well, don't just stare at her. Ask her what she wants."

"I…uh, I'm…what do you want?"

Agnes didn't respond.

"What's she saying?" Thelma asked.

"Nothing. She's just kind of standing there."

Del's entire body stiffened, except for her mouth, which she moved as carefully as possible. "Are you Agnes Hamilton?"

I didn't know if Agnes was ignoring Delphina, or if she couldn't hear her. I would have asked her, but I was too afraid.

"What's she saying? Did she answer?" Thelma asked.

I slowly shook my head.

"Then how do you know it's her?"

"She's wearing a wedding dress and has a rope around her neck."

"Oh, bless her heart. She is real," Thelma said.

"I'd rather see a rat after all," Olivia said.

"Hush, girls. We got a séance going on here. Let Chantilly talk to Agnes."

"She's not responding."

The spirit twirled around in a clip and flew up to the rafter where she'd spent her last moments alive.

My heart pounded and my head burned, yet my entire body shivered from the cold air surrounding me. My vision blurred, and I blinked several times to clear it, but it didn't help. Knots formed in my stomach, and I felt sick, like I wanted to throw up.

Suddenly a scene shaped around me.

A person dressed in black.

A rope.

A knife.

A letter dropping to the ground.

A deep guttural scream.

The stomping of feet, more screaming, arguing.

"No, no. Please, don't," a woman cried.

A beautiful woman with her long hair twisted into an up 'do wearing a stunning, white beaded wedding dress struggled on the wide curved staircase with a person dressed in all black. A suit maybe? The person carried himself like a man but it was too blurry to say for sure. She screamed over and over, begging and pleading for mercy.

"No, no. Please, don't."

The rope swung from the rafter, and the person in black caught it and wrapped it around her neck. She pushed at him, the piece of paper in her hand. She kicked at him, and screamed more.

"No, please. Stop. Why are you doing this to me?"

They wrestled and she fought hard to break free, but he had her arms pinned to her sides with one arm, his grip tight.

"Please, you're hurting me. Please."

She kicked and screamed, but the person in black was too strong for her. He lifted her up, the train of her wedding gown swaying and creeping down the grand staircase, and then heaved her over the railing.

Her arms hung loosely by her sides as the last of the long dress train slowly fell through the railing. A plain white high heeled shoe dropped to the ground as the piece of paper dropped from her hand and slowly followed.

A loud crack echoed through the room, followed by a slow, rhythmic creaking sound, like the kind heard when a floor joint is old and loose. Creak. Creak. Creee-ak.

The fog cleared, and as I peered up at the rafter, I saw her body swinging slowly from it, back and forth, back and forth, her lifeless eyes beating down at me.

Creak. Creak. Creak.

I jerked in my chair. "There. She's right there. Don't y'all see her?"

They fixed their eyes on the rafter, but each of them swore they couldn't see a thing.

Delphina shouted, "Agnes Hamilton, go home You don't belong here anymore."

The spirit just swung back and forth like we weren't even there.

"She can't hear you," I said. "She's gone."

"She disappeared?" Olivia asked.

"No, she died. All over again." Like, I realized, she'd been doing for all these years.

Olivia sighed. "Oh, my."

Thelma nodded. "Goodness. That's just terrible."

"We have to help her," Delphina said.

I gazed up at her swinging body. "Hold on."

They kept their eyes focused on me as I stood and walked over to the stairs and climbed up to where Agnes Hamilton's body hung, an image none of them could see. I reached out toward her lifeless body but I couldn't quite get to her. She seemed so lifelike, so real, like I'd walked into a time warp and found her the moment she'd died. I gazed down for a moment and panicked. The restaurant was no longer a restaurant but a home. A grand, beautiful home with a dead bride-to-be swinging from a rafter.

I had entered into some type of time warp. The room was a glorious entry with wood and marble floors, beautiful paintings hanging on the walls, and incredible furniture with intricate details.

It was Agnes Hamilton's home.

Air rushed past me, and the man—I saw him clear as day and recognized him as male—raced down the stairs. He swiped up the paper that floated to the ground, read it, and then stuffed it into his pants pocket. He glanced up at the rafter, laughed, and walked out the front door.

I ran as fast as I could down those stairs, part of me afraid I'd be stuck in that moment in time, and the other part cursing myself for making my head throb more than it had in hours, but

I needed to follow the man, to find out who he was. Because I knew the truth. Agnes Hamilton didn't kill herself. She was murdered.

Only, when I went through the door, he was gone, and wherever I'd been was gone, too.

I walked back inside, my head hung and my shoulders slumped.

"What happened?" Del asked.

Olivia ran up to me and hugged me. "Oh, Chantilly, where did you go? One minute you were here, and the next you disappeared on the stairs. Heavens, I thought I was going to die."

Thelma adjusted the wrap around her curlers. "Yup, you just up and disappeared in a poof." She accentuated the oof in poof. "My Uncle Henry used to think he could make himself invisible. He'd sit on the couch and say he was going, and then he'd do the most horrific things because he thought we couldn't see him, but we could."

Delphina sighed. "I know I'm going to hate myself for this, but what horrific things did he do?"

"Oh, horrible, terrible things. He would pick his nose and flick the boogers at us, and then he'd scratch himself in the most inappropriate places. It was just terrible."

Delphina stared at Thelma like she always did. "I knew I shouldn't have asked."

That all would have been funny had I not just seen a woman killed a minute before. I shivered but sweated at the same time. I needed to sit. I needed to catch my breath. I sat in my chair and stared up at the rafter, the empty, barren rafter. "I think I went back in time or something. I don't know."

"You went back in time?" Olivia asked.

Delphina remained calm while the other two freaked out. "What did you see?"

"I saw what happened to Agnes. It was like I was right there watching it as it happened, only they couldn't see me."

Thelma raised her eyebrow. "They?"

"She wasn't alone."

Delphina led me back to my chair. "Who was with her?"

"A man, but I couldn't get a good look at his face." As if I would have recognized him anyway. "He…he wrapped the noose around her neck and pushed her. She didn't kill herself." I fell into the chair.

"She was showing you what happened to her," Delphina said. "She wants the truth to be known."

"God rest her soul, maybe she's been trying to tell people all along, and you're the only one that could see her," Thelma said.

My hands shook, and my teeth chattered, neither of which I realized were happening until that moment. "I guess, maybe. I don't know. Maybe I just imagined it."

"Oh sugar, you didn't imagine it. The room was freezing, and I know for a fact the air conditioner doesn't work that well. Bobby was too cheap to replace the darn thing."

"Um, excuse me." Olivia raised her hand. "We're all forgetting one important thing."

"No," I shook my head. "At least I'm not."

"What?" Thelma asked.

I sighed. "Poor Bobby Joe Pruitt. He's not here."

"Well, maybe he went to the other place after all," Thelma said.

My eyes widened, and Olivia gasped.

"That ain't the respectful way to speak of the dead," Del said.

Honestly, I thought she'd burst a blood vessel, so I was quite surprised at her composure.

"She's fixin' to blow but good," Olivia whispered. "Nobody's allowed to say that about her kin except her."

She was right.

I wasn't sure how to handle it. Bobby was family to Del, and even though she knew he wasn't the nicest peanut in the bag, she was the only one left allowed to say that.

"Thelma, God is a forgiving God. If he wasn't, he'd have taken you out years ago."

I glanced at Olivia. She shrugged.

Delphina held back, so I assumed it was out of respect for her unofficially adopted child.

"I, uh...I think we need to do this again," I sat in Delphina's chair. "This time, I'll try." I wasn't sure what I'd seen, if it was my imagination or what not, but I needed to know. "I feel like I'm missing something here." I encouraged them all to sit.

When they did, we all joined hands again, of course, after Delphina gave Thelma a pinch on her forearm.

"Oh, that hurt."

"Was supposed to. That's for saying Bobby's in the other place."

"Okay, I don't know if I need to say anything specific, but I don't care." I bowed my head and then lifted my eyes to everyone. "Please close your eyes and bow your heads."

Once I made sure everyone was in compliance, I took a few deep breaths and prayed I wasn't doing something I shouldn't be then I bowed my head again. I kept my eyes open that time though. "Bobby Joe Pruitt, we'd like to talk to you. We want to know if you're okay, and if you can tell us what happened to you. We want to help you."

Nothing happened. No flash of cold air, no trembling table, no stopping of time, nothing.

"Come on, Bobby. We're trying to help here."

The table vibrated just a bit beneath our hands.

Olivia lifted her head. "Did you feel that?"

"Shh," Delphina said.

Olivia bowed her head again.

"Bobby, is that you?" I asked.

The table shook again ever so slightly, but other than that, nothing happened.

"Bobby Joe Pruitt, you do what your momma taught you, and

you acknowledge someone when they're talking to you, you hear me?" Delphina said.

Nothing.

Everyone lifted their heads and opened their eyes.

"I'm sorry," I said. "I thought maybe it would work."

"Maybe Bobby's not interested in helping. Maybe he just wants to be left alone," Thelma said.

A knife flew through the air and across the room, stabbing and sticking straight into the stair wall.

Olivia screamed, Thelma ducked under the table, and Delphina pushed her chair away and marched over to the knife, pulling it out of the wall. "Looks like Bobby came by after all."

"How did that happen?" Thelma asked.

A knock on the front door set Olivia screaming as she hid under the table with Thelma. It scared me too, sending a rush of panic from the pit of my stomach and up my throat. Del stayed glued to the stairs holding the knife.

I shook away the fear as Del said, "You gonna get that?"

"Uh, I guess?" I slowly walked over to the door. "Who is it?"

"Jack Levitt, ma'am. Castleberry PD. We got a call someone was inside the restaurant."

I breathed a huge sigh of relief and unlocked the door.

When Jack saw my face, he raised his left eyebrow. "Everything okay in here?"

Thelma and Olivia crawled out from under the table. Jack watched and glanced at me. "Bunco night, perhaps?"

I'd never been a Bunco girl. "No. We were just, um...we were just..." I wasn't exactly sure how to explain what we were doing.

"We were calling on Bobby's spirit," Del said. "Trying to figure out who killed him."

Great, I thought. Just what I needed Jack to know. His eyes opened more, and I blushed.

"And what did you find?"

"Uh, we...uh—"

Del waved the knife. "We found this."

Jack climbed up the three stairs to where Delphina stood. He removed a glove from his pocket and I wondered if he always had those on hand. "May I have that?"

Del handed it to him.

"Excuse me, but you should have seen it, Detective Levitt," Olivia said. "It just flew across the room from right over there and stuck into the wall like a pig in mud."

"She's right," Thelma said. "I saw it with my own eyes."

He pursed his lips and crooked his finger at me. "May I see you for a moment? Alone?"

I glanced back at the women as I nodded and followed him outside.

"Care to fill me in here?"

"We aren't breaking any laws. Delphina has a key. If that's what you're wondering, I mean."

"It's an active crime scene. You aren't allowed to be here."

"But the crime happened upstairs. We haven't gone up there." Not yet, anyway, I thought.

A small smile crept over his face.

I smiled, too. I couldn't help myself. He had a cute smile.

"Typically when a crime happens, the entire area is closed off, but since we wrongly assumed no one would enter the restaurant, we didn't tape off the entrances."

"Oh, so we're not—"

He hung his head and shook it. When he looked at me again, the smile was still there. "Were you really trying to summon Bobby Pruitt's spirit?"

I blew out a breath. "Maybe?"

He nodded. "Good grief. Y'all are a hot mess, aren't you?"

"In my defense, it was Delphina's idea, and it's really hard to say no to that woman."

"Especially when she's pushing hard. That's why I went out with Lonna in the first place."

Delphina set them up? "I didn't know that."

"The woman is a powerful force when she wants to be."

"So you understand why I'm here?"

"I understand that woman gets what she wants when she pushes, but a séance? That's a little over the top."

"She wants to know what happened to Bobby."

"Chantilly, if that stuff worked, police departments all over the world would be using psychics to help solve cases."

"I know some do. There's that woman just a few counties south of here that works with the Atlanta police. I read about her in the newspaper when I visited my parents a while back."

He laughed. "I think I know who you're talking about, but I'm not convinced those kinds of people are the real thing."

"We just thought the séance might help, and we wanted to do it for Del." I breathed heavily, feeling deflated and a bit embarrassed.

"Well, did it?"

"Help?" If he considered my seeing Agnes Hamilton's death and knowing it wasn't a suicide, yes, it did, but I wasn't prepared to have that discussion. "Not really, except the knife. It honestly did fly across the room."

He flipped the knife in his hand and examined it. "Probably just fell off the table."

"And flew several feet through the air and stuck itself into the wall?" I opened the front door. All three women fell forward, obviously listening to our conversation. "Besides, it wasn't even on the table. No utensils are on the table."

"It's true," Delphina said. "Look how far it went." She walked over to the area the knife came from. "From here." She walked to the stair where it landed on the wall, counting each step along the way. "That's twenty-six steps. There's no way that knife would slip and go that far, let alone pass over our heads and over the railing like it did. Especially since it came flat out of nowhere." She straightened her shoulders. "It was Bobby trying to talk to us."

"With a knife? Maybe someone else was here and you didn't see them?"

"How could they be? I locked the door behind us."

"Could they have come in another way?"

Delphina rubbed her chin. "I guess through the cellar, but they would have had to walk by us to get behind us, so I don't see how that's possible."

"It was a ghost," Thelma said.

"It wasn't a ghost. Ghosts can't throw things." He opened his mouth and closed it, and then a second later said, "I can't believe I even said that."

"How do you know that? One time my Charlie came by for a visit. I'd left his favorite pillow on the couch because I like to nap on it. It reminds me of him. I went into the kitchen for lunch, and when I came back, the pillow was on his recliner again where he liked it."

"We thought he'd come through to Chantilly like Agnes did, but he didn't," I said.

Jack's eyes shifted to mine. I shrugged and looked away. "Well, whatever's happening here, this is an active crime scene, and I need you all to get on home, okay?"

Olivia perked up, and I knew she was relieved. "You mean we're not under arrest?"

"No, ma'am. You're free to go home."

She pressed her hand to her chest. "Oh, thank heaven for that. I didn't want to upset my family name by being a common criminal."

"Bless her heart," Delphina said. She attempted to blow out the candles, but there were a lot of them. "Can I get a little help here?"

Olivia darted back to the table. She'd been carefully making her way toward the entrance, I assumed to skedaddle as quickly as possible. "Oh, yes. I'll help. I have stronger breath because of my age."

Del just shook her head. I was actually quite proud of her. She hadn't tipped over the edge the entire night. Lord knew she'd had plenty of opportunities.

They blew out each candle with Thelma on their tail gathering them up and stuffing them into a small box. Where the box came from, I had no idea.

"Ladies, did any of you drive here?"

"No, sir. We met at Delphina's café and walked from there," Olivia said.

He nodded. "Did anyone drive there?"

Everyone said no.

"Then come on, it's late. I'll drive you all home." He popped the door open, and after we'd made sure we had everything, he let us out, one by one, Delphina last. "You've got the key?"

She nodded and handed it to him. He closed the door and locked it.

After dropping them all off, we headed to my house. "So you want to give me any more details?"

Not really, I thought. "I already told you. Delphina had this crazy idea to perform the séance, and she corralled us all to go along with her. We thought it would make her feel better. That's about it."

He glanced at me and then back at the road ahead of us. "You sure?"

"What do you mean?"

"Maybe you're not telling me something because you don't want me to know?"

"Other than the knife flying through the air for no reason? I don't think so."

He shook his head. "I wouldn't put it past Delphina to mess with y'all like that, especially those two. You sure you weren't playing along with her?"

"Jack, how do you think we could have messed around with Olivia and Thelma? We aren't magicians. We can't make things appear in thin air." I adjusted the seatbelt. "Or fly through it, for that matter." I made a tsk sound like my mother used to when I'd said something ludicrous. "You don't have to believe any of us, but we know the truth. Besides, there's been rumors of that place being haunted for years now."

"I don't believe in ghosts," he said.

"That doesn't mean they aren't real."

"Okay." He pulled into my driveway, pacifying me with his dismissive comment.

I glanced at Austin's dark bedroom. At least he was asleep.

"Listen, something's come up, and we need to discuss it."

"Okay?"

He clicked the locks on his door and the car doors unlocked. "May I come in for a few minutes?"

I checked my watch. It was almost eleven o'clock. I had no idea how it had gotten that late. "Uh, I need to be up for work in the morning."

"It's police business, Chantilly."

"Oh, well then, sure. Come on in." I stepped out of the vehicle and closed the door behind me. "What's going on?" I unlocked the front door. "Would you like something to drink?" Cooper wandered over and rubbed up on my leg. I stooped and gave him a pat on the head.

"I'm good, thanks."

"So, what's going on?"

"I spoke to the hostess from the restaurant again. She said you and Bobby had an argument about something? She said Bobby was pretty upset and Delphina had to intervene."

I pulled my left foot under my right leg and got comfortable on the couch. "If by intervene, you mean stop Bobby from being his usual self then yes, that's what happened."

He didn't take his eyes off me. "Can you tell me about the argument?"

"It...it was nothing really. He wanted to make some architectural changes to the restaurant, and I told him he'd have to get approval. I might have mentioned I wasn't sure he'd get it but I really...I can't remember. What's going on, Jack?"

"We're looking into the suspects, that's all."

"Are you saying I'm a suspect?"

His eyes shifted toward the hallway but then back to me. "I'm saying Bobby had issues with a lot of people in town, and someone saw him arguing with you."

My entire body tensed. "I didn't kill him."

"I'm not saying you did. I'm a detective, Chantilly. This is my job, questioning everyone involved in the case."

"And since someone said Bobby argued with me—I didn't argue with him—I'm involved in the case?"

"You're involved in the case because you discovered his body and because the cooks said Bobby argued with you." He stood up and examined the photos on the wall. "I don't think you killed him, Chantilly. But I have a job to do, and I have to do it."

"I know."

I relaxed on the couch after Jack left. I didn't turn on the TV or leave a light on. I just needed peace and quiet. Cooper settled onto my chest and breathed his kitty breath in my face. I tried to relax, but I couldn't stop thinking about what was happening to me.

Maybe the fall had done something after all. None of the women saw what I saw, and I knew it wasn't my imagination. Too many things had been happening lately, and all of them after falling down the stairs. I could have jarred something in my brain when it smacked into the marble floor. I'd heard of things like that happening, brain shifts that caused blackouts and hallucinations. Oh dear, was that my issue? Was I having hallucinations?

So much for relaxing.

It didn't matter, at least not then. What mattered was Bobby Pruitt's murder. Whether Jack wanted to say it outright or not, I was on his suspect list. He said the only concern was bad timing on my part. His body temperature told the story, he said, and Bobby's death had occurred only minutes before I'd said I arrived.

I needed to figure out who killed Bobby. For Austin, I needed to do it for Austin. The last thing that poor child needed was his mother being accused of murder. He'd already gone through so much.

He deserved better. He deserved stability and structure for a change. The last year hadn't been much of that, and we'd only recently begun to find our place, get our rhythm, and I didn't want that disrupted. Of course, I didn't want that disrupted.

I'd explained that to Jack before he left. I'd even told him about Jesse and Julia Lye, and Rashid Patel, and the issues they'd each had with Bobby. I knew Del would vouch for me, but I didn't care. I needed to figure out what happened to Bobby so there was no question in my son's mind.

He promised to talk to Maybelle Parker, and I knew our meeting on the street would verify when I arrived, but still, I worried something would go wrong.

Because that's how things had gone for me over the past year. Wrong. And that wasn't because of some tumble down a few stairs.

CHAPTER 6

"No, no. Please, don't. I won't tell anyone. Josiah, please, no."

I opened my eyes. The room was dark, just as it was when Jack left. I grabbed my phone from the coffee table and checked the time. Three o'clock. I'd fallen asleep on the couch, Cooper lying on my chest, too, until I woke with a start from a dream. Actually, a nightmare. I jolted awake and Cooper took off for a peaceful, less jumpy place to sleep.

I'd dreamed of Agnes Hamilton. Her long hair falling from its beautifully styled up 'do, tangling in the rope twisted around her neck. Her voice cracking as she cried, begging and screaming for help, pleading with Josiah. Oh my goodness, Josiah. Of course. Her fiancé. He's the one. The one in black. The one who killed her.

Cooper kneaded my legs. I picked him up from my lap and set him on the small throw on the other side of the couch. "Agnes," I whispered, as if she'd actually answer me. She wanted me to know, wanted me to see what happened to her. I knew it like I knew the sun would rise every day. I just didn't know what I was supposed to do about it. "What can I do?"

Frustrated, I got up and walked to the kitchen with Cooper on my tail. I poured myself a glass of water, took my vitamins, shut off the light over the sink, and then shuffled to my room. Instead of doing my regular nightly ritual, I quickly washed my face, brushed my teeth, and changed my clothes. I fell into bed, exhausted. I couldn't stop thinking about Agnes Hamilton and her fiancé Josiah. My mind raced as my body begged for slumber, but it just wouldn't come.

I watched the clock on my nightstand hit four, four-forty-seven, and almost every minute until six o'clock when it was time to start the day. I sat up, not at all prepared for what the day would bring, and not at all rested.

———

"Did he kiss you?"

Thelma sighed. "I remember my first kiss. It was Wilbur Harris. We were walking in the park, and he told me he wanted to marry me. He kissed me, and it was the most awful thing."

Her story surprised Del. "I thought Charlie was your first kiss?"

"Oh, heavens no. I was seven when I had my first kiss. Charlie was my second. We were in high school. I remember the day like it was yesterday. We'd been—"

"Not now, Thelma. We're getting the dirt on Chantilly."

They joined forces to bombard me with questions about Jack Levitt driving me home after our adventure the night before. I'd considered skipping my coffee stop that morning, but after my limited sleep, I definitely needed the caffeine boost. "He basically told me I'm a suspect in Bobby's murder."

Both of them sat there with their mouths hanging open.

Del broke the silence first. "He what?"

"I was the last one to see Bobby alive, so it just makes sense that I'd be the one to kill him, and considering the hostess said she saw us arguing, I'm a shoo-in for the murder."

"But I was there. I saw Bobby start the argument, and I know you didn't argue back."

"I know, and I'm hoping you'll say that to Detective Levitt."

"Oh. It's Detective Levitt now?" Thelma asked.

"It's his job."

"But you went on a date."

"No, we went to dinner, with my son. That's not a date."

"It's how the divorced date." She sipped her coffee. "That's what I read in an article in Cosmo magazine."

"You read Cosmo?" Del snorted. "What in the devil do you do that for?"

"It's important to keep up on the latest fashion trends."

"Honey, Dolly Parton wigs aren't a fashion trend. If Cosmo ain't saying that, it's time to read something else."

It was the perfect moment to mention Lonna to Del. "Oh, Jack told me you pushed him to go out with Lonna."

The door to the café swung open.

Thelma clapped her hands and giggled. "Look, you are psychic."

Lonna Appleton pranced through the door like she owned the place.

I whispered to the group. "I wouldn't call me psychic because of her."

Lonna smirked and greeted us with a condescending, "Ladies." She strutted over, dragged a chair out from beneath our table and sat. Uninvited. "Chantilly, you're just the person I wanted to see." She removed her phone from her purse, tapped an app open, then held it up toward me. "I understand you were the last person to see Bobby Pruitt and are now a key suspect for the investigation. Care to comment on that?"

Delphina grabbed the phone from Lonna's hand. "She is innocent. I was with her during that argument with Bobby. He confronted her, and she didn't argue back at all. She was professional and courteous and said she'd do what she could to help him, and I'm sure that's just what she did. You might could talk to the others in the barbecue competition, 'cause they ought to be suspects, too."

Lonna yanked the phone from Del's hand. "Miss Beauregard, thank you for your comments." Her voice shook ever so slightly. Lonna knew she'd treaded dangerous waters coming to Community Café like that. Delphina wasn't above the law by any means, but the café was almost a sanctuary spot for everyone in town. It was a place of peace, comfort food, sweet tea, and conversation, unless you ticked off the owner. Then all bets were off, but the only person allowed to raise their voice or start any kind of discord there was Delphina herself.

I cringed from the glare Del shot Lonna. I actually felt bad for the woman even though she had a long wild hair up her behind about me.

I leaned toward my high school annoyance, prepared to battle her with a strong defensive strategy. Okay, I didn't have a strategy per say, but I hoped if I was kind and firm, she'd be respectful. "Lonna, I'm happy to speak to you, if you'll report the facts."

She crossed her legs. "Oh sweetie, I'm all about reporting the facts, of course. And the facts are, you're the last person to see Bobby Joe Pruitt, and you two had a confrontation the night before. So, what say you?"

"I say you're wrong."

Lonna's confident stare, her raised eyebrow, and straight lined lips didn't falter. She just kept her phone in her hand pointed toward my face.

"You're wrong. There is no proof, just assumption, that I was the last person to see Bobby for one, and we did not have a confrontation the night before. Bobby was simply being Bobby. Argumentative and bullish, just like he was in high school, remember?" I crossed my arms over my chest, satisfied I'd tamed the bear beside me. I just hoped it worked on her, too.

It didn't. She didn't falter. "My source tells me you were upset when you left, that Delphina had to drag you out of here, and that your emotions were high. What about—"

Delphina slammed her hand down on the table. "That's a bunch of podunk, and you know it. She was doing her job, and that's it. I told you what happened. I was there. Whoever your source is is lying like a dog on a rug, and you can quote me on that." She adjusted her pink and white apron. "Now you listen here, Lonna Appleton. Your momma and me, we've been friends a long time, and I know she would tan your hide for acting like this without knowing everything. So you get out of my café, and you go and find the truth, and that's what you report. The truth, not some gossip about an innocent woman you don't like because your boyfriend's been making oogly eyes at her."

The rest of the patrons in the café stared at all of us. No one said a word. Lonna's chin nearly hit the floor.

Thelma, who'd been sitting there silently the entire time, coughed and said, "I'll make my column a testament to your innocence." She patted my hand and whispered, "Are you sure you didn't kill him?"

"Yes, I'm sure." I should have elaborated, at least for Lonna's articles sake, but I was too worried on the can of worms Delphina had just popped open, and how badly I'd hoped it would stay shut. Jack hadn't exactly made oogly eyes at me anyway.

Lonna glanced around the room at the customers gawking at us. She slowly set the phone down on the table and stared at it for a moment. "I don't know what you're talking about, and I'm just doing my job." Lonna made eye contact with me again. "I'm an honest reporter, and I'll report what I am told. If it's factual, and I can prove it, of course I'll note that. If however, it's hearsay,

I'll also mention that, but I'll still report it, because the people have a right to know."

I shook my head. "You do what you have to do."

Thelma wiggled her finger in a disapproving motion. "Oh, that's not good. That might could upset Detective Levitt, and I don't think you want that."

Del snorted. "Don't matter none anyway. The minute that detective laid eyes on our pretty Chantilly, Lonna didn't have a chance."

Lonna's face burned red. She stuffed her phone into her purse and stood. "I believe we're done here."

Delphina yelled at Lonna's back as she pranced out the café's door, "You're lucky I don't ban you from coming back."

The ten or so people in the café still hadn't moved. I honestly thought they were afraid to. Delphina stood and glanced around the place. "What're y'all starin' at?" She marched back behind the counter and got to work.

Her patrons carried on, most likely out of fear.

I buried my head in my hands. "Dear God, this is the last thing my son needs."

Thelma patted my back. "There, there now, honey. We'll fix this. Your momma is watching over you, and that woman won't let a thing happen to you."

I dragged my fingers down my face. I noticed they didn't slide as easily as they used to, but instead got caught in a wrinkle or two. I'd aged years in a single one, and being accused of murder would only add to that, I thought. "I didn't kill Bobby."

Thelma continued rubbing my back, and it comforted me. "Of course you didn't. It just looks like you did."

"Zip it, woman," Delphina said. She smiled at me. "We'll fix this. The real killer is out there, and we'll find him."

"I'm not an investigator. I don't have a clue how to do that."

"Don't worry. I got it covered. We'll talk to the other suspects and get the truth out of one of them."

"And just how to you expect to do that?" I asked.

Thelma squeezed my hand. "I don't think we really want to know."

"Well, we ain't going to torture them, if that's what you think. At least not like they used to back in the day, anyway."

Thelma bit her bottom lip and her top teeth popped out and fell into her cup of coffee.

I glanced up at Delphina, whose eyes bulged out of her head. We both busted out laughing as Thelma stuffed her teeth back into place.

"Quit laughin'. I need to get me some more teeth glue. Ran out last week."

"Em hmm," Del said.

"If you keep at it, I'm going to talk to you like this the rest of my life." She pulled the top teeth partially out and said, "What do you think?"

It came out more like "But bo bou bhink?"

She smiled and the teeth popped out again and we all laughed.

"Thank you," I said. "I needed that."

Olivia walked through the café door. "Oh, my goodness, someone lit a fire under Lonna Appleton's behind, and that woman has done lost her mind."

I grabbed Delphina's hand and waved it. "That would be Del."

Olivia sat across from me and slouched her shoulders. "What happened?"

We filled her in.

"Oh heavens, you couldn't murder someone. Lord, everyone that knows you knows that."

Thelma sipped her coffee. "Lonna's just trying to frame her on account of that detective having the hots for her and all."

"He does not have the hots for me."

They all stared at me. I shifted in my seat, and the room heated up ten degrees. "He doesn't."

Delphina pointed at Thelma. "And that one there's got a genius IQ."

Thelma smiled. "I wouldn't say it's genius, but it's close. I did get all satisfactory marks in school."

"See?" Delphina took a small notebook from her apron pocket. "Okay, who we got?"

"For what?" Thelma asked.

"For suspects?"

"Oh, that. Yes."

I sighed and listed out the possibilities. "I hate to say it, but it could be anyone competing in the competition, and that's a pretty large list."

"Sixty-five booths to be exact," Olivia said.

Thelma shook her head. "Oh goodness. That's a lot of people. What can we do?"

"We start with the ones we know had motive." I dug through my work bag and found a pen and blank pad of paper. I always kept an extra one in my bag. "Okay, we had two competitors come to the meeting, Jesse and Julia Lye, and Rashid Patel." I wrote down their names. "And then there's Maybelle."

Olivia gasped. "Maybelle? Maybelle Parker? I just can't see her hurting someone. She's so sweet."

"It's always the ones we least expect," Del said.

Thelma backed her chair away from me.

"She doesn't mean me, Thelma."

"Well, you're the one I'd least expect."

"She must have hit the ground when her momma birthed her," Del said.

I tapped the pen on the table. "Del."

She shrugged. "I'm just saying."

Thelma pulled out her top teeth and smiled at Del, but Del waved her hand in Thelma's face and turned away.

"I can go through the list of competitors," Olivia said, "but most of them are in it for the fun, not because they really want to win. It's more of a big party for most of them."

Del agreed. "Only a few take it seriously."

"What you need to do is talk to Bobby. Get him to tell you who knocked him off," Thelma said.

"We tried that, and I am not participating in another séance. I don't like what happened to me for starters, and I don't want to get anyone else in trouble, namely all of you."

"Besides, Bobby didn't show himself," Olivia said. "And Miss Chantilly shouldn't be doing things like that anymore. She doesn't need any of this stress with her concussion."

"I'm fine sweetie, really." Fine other than hearing whispers that sounded an awful lot like my parents, seeing a dead woman and the person I thought might have actually killed her, oh, and being a murder suspect, of course. Yup, I was completely fine.

Who was I kidding? I was a hot mess, and I needed to do something. "There's a lacrosse game tonight, maybe the Lye's truck will be there. I can check."

Thelma offered to tag along. "I'm good at getting the truth from people. Look at how honest I've kept Delphina here. She would lie like a rug everyday if it wasn't for me."

Del snarled. "What in the devil are you even talking about?"

"I keep you honest and wholesome. We're like that moon thingie the hippies all used to have hanging on their doors in the 60s and 70s."

Del shook her head. "Moon thingie? Nothing this woman says ever makes any sense."

Olivia raised her hand. "Excuse me, but they're not moons, at least I don't think that's what she means. I think she means yin and yang. You two complement each other. I studied it in my philosophy class in college."

"What'd you take that garbage for?"

"Del." I used my stern mom voice on her. I wasn't afraid of Del. I knew under that cantankerous jaded shell beat a heart of gold. She couldn't fool me. "As a wise woman once said, zip it, woman."

"Oh no." Thelma gripped the table with her wrinkled hands. "Better hold on there, Olivia. The tornado's a comin'."

I smirked at Del and held my finger to my lips. "Shh." I needed to get to work, as did Olivia, so we quickly developed a plan of action, and part of that included me talking to Jack Levitt about the suspects. I didn't know if he'd be at the ball game later, but I highly doubted it with a murder investigation on his hands. In the meantime though, I had to get started proving my innocence and figure out what was happening to me.

CHAPTER 7

I locked myself up in my office, explaining to Olivia I had to catch up on some things and would prefer to not be disturbed. She promised to handle the three small tours, one being a kindergarten class from the local school, and not bother me unless it was necessary.

"Can you do me a favor though, when you have the time of course?"

"Yes, ma'am."

"Can you do some research on Josiah Dilts? I'd like to know what happened to him."

Olivia nodded. "Sure thing. I'll get to it between tours."

"Thank you."

I stared at my internet search engine, digging back into the recesses of my brain for any details I could recall about the murder of the young parents in a neighboring county a few years back. I knew the medium that figured it out was nearby, I just couldn't remember her name.

When I couldn't recall too much of it, I typed what I could into my computer and up popped several articles.

Arrest made in young mother that called 911 prior to being shot

The case was solved by a special investigator named Aaron Banner with the assistance of a local psychic, but her name wasn't mentioned in the article. Interesting, I thought, because I remembered reading about it when it happened. I searched further and finally entered psychic medium, Atlanta Georgia area, and up came Angela Panther in several articles about investigations over the few years since that murder. The last article I read said she didn't speak publicly of her gift, but had been a key tool used by Banner and other officers in several investigations.

I wondered if Angela Panther bumped her head and then struggled with strange, ghostly visions? I didn't have any other explanation. I knew I didn't make up Agnes Hamilton, and I knew I hadn't imagined my father's voice or seeing him in my dream. I just didn't know what to do about any of it.

I needed advice.

Angel Panther didn't have a website, a Facebook page or an Instagram account, and there wasn't anything on LinkedIn for her either. Of course, if I did what she did, and I didn't want it to be bothered, I would have kept off social media completely, too.

I checked for Aaron Banner and found he'd recently taken a job with the Georgia Bureau of Investigations. After a lot of digging and a tense call with someone on their tip line, I finally left a message for him. I stumbled over my words, but said I was looking for the psychic he'd worked with, and that I thought I might have a similar thing—my exact word—and I saw something, but I didn't know what to do about it. When I realized what that sounded like, I assured him it was from over one hundred years ago, and I just wanted to talk to someone that might be able to walk me through it. I apologized for sounding insane, and I didn't mention I might be a suspect in a recent murder because I didn't want to lose any credibility I might have had left.

I went on with my day, and when it came time for Austin's lacrosse game, and I hadn't heard back from Detective Banner or the psychic medium, I'd figured he'd just deleted my message.

I stopped at Delphina's on my way to Austin's game. She'd pushed four tables together, leaving one table for patrons, and had papers spread out all over them. She and Thelma argued over what papers went where.

Thelma placed a paper on top of another one. "That one goes next to this guy."

"You put those two next to each other, and we'll have a brawl before the competitions over."

I examined the papers, all of which were contestant applications. "I thought it was mostly a fun event?"

Del smiled. "Oh, it ain't the competition they fight about."

"Then why the brawl?"

"One's a Bama fan, and the other went to Auburn."

"Oh, boy. Keep them as far apart as possible." I swiped the paper and handed it to Thelma. "You know better than that, woman."

She snatched it from my hand. "'Course I do. It's just fun to watch them get all out a sorts about a silly game with a funny shaped ball."

I raised my eyebrow. She was probably the only person in Castleberry, Georgia, and perhaps the entire South, to call it a silly game. "If you say so."

Delphina placed the application on top of another one. "It's settled. I'm the head judge in this thing, and I want to taste all the barbecue. I don't eat for two days to prepare for this. I don't want these two killing each other before the competition starts." She covered her mouth with her hand. "Oh Lawd, that wasn't what I meant."

"Yes, it was, but it's okay. We all know you didn't mean it the wrong way."

Thelma shook her head back and forth slowly. "I'm not so sure."

"You still planning to come with me to the lacrosse game?"

She nodded. "Bought me one of those cushions for the bleachers, too. So my little bum doesn't get sore."

Del lifted her eyes to Thelma. "You got enough cushion of your own, you don't need to be buying none."

"My granddaughter tells me thick is in these days. No one likes a skinny Minnie."

"Del, what's your plan for the evening? Would you like to come?"

She shook her head. "I'm meeting the cooks at Bobby's."

"But I thought we weren't allowed in there?"

"Detective Jack said they've pretty much done all they can there, and as long as we stay in the kitchen it's okay. We got business to attend to at the restaurant, and I'm the one Bobby left in charge, so I've got to get to it."

"Are you planning to keep the place open?"

She shrugged. "Don't know yet, but I figured it would be a good time to talk to the cooks and see what they have to say about the day he died."

I appreciated that, and I made sure to tell her.

She poured my iced coffee in a to-go cup and added a splash of cream, just the way I liked it. "It's the right thing to do. I know you didn't kill Bobby, and I know his momma would want me to make sure the truth is out."

I understood. "If I can help, please let me know."

She swung her chin toward Thelma. "You're helping by getting that old woman off my hands."

"Give her a break. We're all she's got."

Delphina winked. "She wouldn't like me any other way."

I suspected she was right.

As we were about to leave, Rashid Patel entered the café. "Hello ladies. How are you doing today?"

Del gave him a discontented look I assumed was meant to express her current emotional state.

"Oh, hello, Mr. Patel. I like your shirt. It's very yellow," Thelma said. "Yellow is my favorite color. It reminds me of my old cat, Buster."

"That's very kind of you. Was your cat yellow like my shirt?"

"Oh, no, no. He was a sprayer. Peed on everything in the house and turned it all yellow."

Del laughed. I had to look away to stop myself from laughing, too.

"Did you come for coffee?" Del finally asked. "I can put on another pot right quick."

"No, no. It is fine. I came to invite you to my restaurant. I want to offer my condolences for the death of your friend. I would like to give you a discount on my barbecue."

Del pursed her lips. "Just a discount?"

"Del, hush," I whispered. I smiled at Rashid Patel. "Excuse her, she's having a hard day. And we appreciate the offer, but we can't tonight."

He nodded. "Yes, yes. That is fine. I am wondering if you know when the location will be up for lease? I am rearranging my plans for my new location, and would like to rent Hamilton House."

Del cocked her head. "It ain't up for lease."

He grimaced. "Oh, I was told Mr. Pruitt was considering selling before his untimely death, but I cannot afford such a large payment just now. I would prefer to lease it and purchase it at a later date."

"Who told you Bobby was considering selling?" she asked.

Rashid cleared his throat. "I, uh...I...I'm sorry. I must be mistaken."

Delphina leaned toward him and bared her teeth. "You're right. You're mistaken. Bobby would never sell Hamilton House. Whoever told you that is lying."

He nodded several times and stepped backward toward the door as he did. "I'm very sorry. Very sorry."

"Go on, get out of here with those lies. Bobby's soul needs to rest in peace." There were a few people standing around watching the scene, and when Delphina noticed, her anger tipped further over the edge. "What're you all staring at? Don't you got nothing better to do than rubberneck a grieving soul?"

Two of the customers turned around and talked to each other. The others scattered out the door quickly.

"Don't know who's saying Bobby wanted to sell the place. He'd never do that. Don't know what's come over people these days. Can't let the dead rest in peace like they ought to." She mumbled on as Thelma rubbed her shoulder. "Now quit that. I ain't no charity case. I don't need anyone feeling sorry for me. Go on, get out of here and do what you're supposed to do. Let me take care of things on my end."

Thelma and I headed to the lacrosse fields knowing how upset Delphina was, but also understanding the last thing she needed was us to make things worse.

Thelma's stomach growled as we turned toward the park. "I'm starving. Those itty bitty sandwiches Del serves aren't made for a woman like me. I need real food. Can we stop at the McDonald's? I would like a whopper and some of those fries."

"That's Burger King, and I don't think there's one in any of the surrounding counties."

"No wonder I can't beat this craving."

I laughed. "We'll just get us some barbecue from the truck. It's the perfect excuse to talk to Jesse and Julia."

"See? I knew I'd be a help."

I met Austin on our side of the field and wished him luck. As I expected, Jack wasn't there. I imagined it was tough being a coach and a cop, but it was nice that a man with such commitment worked to do both.

Thelma and I set our seats down on the first row of bleachers.

Since she was a bit older and a little wobbly in her walk, I didn't want her navigating the cement stairs any higher than that. I struggled with them at times, especially on sunny evenings, and I didn't want something to happen to her because she'd offered to support me. That was the last thing I needed weighing heavily on my heart.

Thelma bounced on her toes. "Oh dear, I've got to use the ladies room."

"Okay, it's close by. Follow me." My cell phone vibrated in my pocket on our way. The caller ID said unknown caller.

I received at least ten telemarketing calls a day, and don't get me started on what happened during an election. I hit the button on the side of my iPhone twice to disconnect the call and held onto Thelma's frail arm as we walked together toward the restrooms.

It buzzed again. I checked and it was the same number. "Go ahead and get it," Thelma said. "I'm going to be a minute. It's never quick anymore."

I smiled. "I'll be right out here." I answered the call. "No, I didn't sign up for your brace information, and I'm too young for a Medicare plan, so please take me off your list."

"Is this Chantilly Adair?"

"Can you please take me—"

"I was given your number by Detective Banner with the GBI. My name is Angela Panther."

I almost dropped the phone. "Oh my gosh, Miss Panther. I'm sorry. I'm Chantilly. I just get so many telemarketing calls, I figured—"

She stopped me before I could finish. "Don't sweat it. I keep my phone on do not disturb for everyone but my contacts for that very reason. And every so often, I mute my daughter's calls too, but that's an entirely different conversation meant for another time."

I laughed. I liked her already. "Thank you for calling. I'm sure my message to the detective sounded strange, but the whole thing is strange."

"Totally get it. If you're experiencing anything like I did then you're probably ready to jump out of your skin. Do you have some time to talk?"

I glanced at the door to the public restrooms. "A few minutes at least."

"Okay, why don't you give me the Reader's Digest version of what's going on? Maybe I can give you my thoughts."

"Okay, well, I think a spirit's trying to tell me how she was killed."

"Has she shown herself to you?"

"Yes, ma'am, in a matter of speaking, at least."

"What does in a matter of speaking mean?"

"I've seen things and then a few friends of mine and I recently held a séance and she showed me what happened to her, but I don't know if I was just watching or what. It's very confusing."

"You held a séance? Have you done that before?"

"No, but it wasn't my idea. A friend insisted, and when she insists, it's hard to say no."

"I have a similar friend. But if she suggests it again, stay strong. Séances open portals, and if you don't know how to close them, you never know who's going to stick around."

"How will I know if I did that?"

"When did you have the séance?"

"Last night."

"You'd know by now."

I took that as a good sign. "I think I'm okay. At least so far."

"That's good, but trust me on that. So, are you seeing what happened like playing out in front of you, or was it like a play and you were a character?"

"It was playing out in front of me. I think."

"Is this the first time this has happened to you?"

"Yes. No. I mean, lately things have been happening, but not to that degree, and none of it started until a few days ago."

"Has something happened recently that would give you an emotional connection to the other side? Maybe you lost a loved one or something?"

I sighed. "My parents both died recently."

She breathed in. "I'm sorry for your loss."

"Thank you."

"Sometimes when we lose people we love, we open up spiritually to the possibilities of things we didn't think about before. It helps us feel a connection to them still, and for people like me, and now, it sounds like you, we realize we have a gift."

"I also fell down the stairs at work and gave myself a concussion."

She laughed. "That could do it, too."

"There's something else."

"There always is."

"A man in town was killed recently, and it looks like I might have been the last person to see him alive."

"Did you do it?"

"No, of course not, but it's important I find out who did. I don't want this upsetting my son. We just moved back to my hometown after my divorce. He doesn't need anything else on his plate right now.

"I understand. But the dead, they like to keep us on our toes."

"What do you mean?"

"I mean a spirit doesn't always just sit down over a cup of coffee and fill us in on the gory details. They like to make things a little harder than that."

"Great. As if this wasn't impossible enough."

"Let me guess, the guy was killed in the same location as the woman you saw?"

"Yes, ma'am. How did you know that?"

"I've been doing this a while. I see the patterns now. And she came through, but he didn't."

"Yes."

"When did she pass?"

"The late 1800s."

"Oh, good grief. She needs to move on."

Angela Panther was funny. "I get the sense that she's not much interested in that."

"Not yet, but that's because she's been trying to find someone to tell her story to. Now that she's got you, I suspect she won't be around much longer."

"But I can't do anything for her."

"Sure you can. You can set the story straight and send her on her way."

I fell back against the outer wall of the restrooms. "I don't know how to do that." I gasped. "I...I just..."

Angela Panther laughed again. "I'm sorry. I don't mean to laugh at you because I've been there. I could write the book on freaking out about helping the dead, but trust me, the sooner you realize you've got a new, unpaying but extremely emotionally satisfying job, you'll adjust."

"I think I'm a bit overwhelmed."

Her tone softened. "You are, and that's okay. Baby steps. That's what my psychic counselor told me, and she was right. Tell me what happened with Agnes. It's my experience that there's always more to what they're telling us than what we think or can figure out in the heat of the moment. When I was a newbie like you, it took me a long time to see the forest through the trees, so I'm sure I can help you navigate this."

"How did you know her name was Agnes?"

She laughed again. "I have a gift, remember?"

Lord, I did not know how things worked, but I took a deep breath and filled her in on exactly what happened.

"So none of the stories about Agnes's death ever mentioned a knife?"

"No, ma'am. Not a one."

"Chantilly—great name by the way—how old are you?"

"Forty-five, why?"

"I'm not a heck of a lot older than you, and I'm not from the South, so you don't have to call me ma'am. Please don't. It makes me feel so old."

"Yes, ma—Angela."

"Okay, let me see if I've got this straight. Agnes Hamilton was obviously hanged—hung—let's just say killed, I can never figure out the right word—by someone in black, and Bobby Pruitt was stabbed, and you saw the person in black in a vision in his office, yes, too?"

"Yes—" I stopped myself before calling her ma'am. "And I can't differentiate the two. They appeared to be the same person, but that can't be possible because the person in black who killed Agnes Hamilton was her fiancé, Josiah Dilts."

"I doubt it's the same person. It's more a frame of reference for Agnes. She's showing you something that happened to her and connecting to what happened to your current spirit. The problem with that is we don't know if the person was actually there when your guy was killed, of if Agnes is showing you something that means something entirely different."

I sighed. "This is too much for me to understand."

"It's definitely over your pay grade for now, but you'll catch on quickly. I can tell that about you."

"So, what am I supposed to do, just guess?

"Communicating with spirits is different for everyone. You'll need to set some ground rules, and I can get you some information to learn how to do that. But it's also important to understand how they're communicating with you, that it's a puzzle that, a lot of times, is pieces that reflect something in your life so you can understand it easier."

"I don't understand any of it."

"That happens, too."

I laughed just as Thelma walked out. "You talking to Delphina?" She pulled her teeth out and smiled. "Take one of those phone camera pictures of me and her. Tell her I said hi."

I held the phone away from my head. "No, it's someone else. Have a seat on the bench for a minute, okay? We'll head over to the food truck in a bit."

She waddled over to the bench and fanned herself after she hollered at a middle aged man to give her a hand. He eased her down onto the bench.

"Sorry about that," I said to Ms. Panther.

"No worries. It does sound to me like there's a message in there from Agnes about Bobby's death, too. The trick is figuring out what it is."

"I don't have any idea how to do that."

"I'll see if I can get anything out of Bobby, but the truth is, he may be at peace, and he's not coming back. It happens often."

"Even though he was murdered?"

"Things like that don't always matter. And then you've got those spirits that are intent on telling their fourth cousin twice removed where they left their silver dollar collection. I swear, the things I've had to tell people."

Oh heavens, I hoped I wouldn't be called upon to do anything like that.

She offered a handful of options on how to proceed, and asked for my email and that I call her in a day or two.

"Who was that? I'm so hungry sitting here, I could eat my own arm."

"I don't think so." I helped her up. "Your arms don't have enough meat to satisfy even a mouse."

"Do mice eat people? I was thinking about getting one of those gerbil things as a pet, but now maybe I should rethink that."

Bless her heart. Thelma was as sweet as they came, but just one can short of a six pack. "Sweetie, a gerbil won't eat you, I promise."

"Maybe I'll just get a cat."

I didn't have the heart to tell her that if something did happen to her she was better off with the gerbil.

As we walked over to the Lye BBQ food truck I told her about my talk with Angela Panther.

"Oh, how exciting." She rubbed her frail hands together. "Does that mean we're going to get to meet a real live psychic?"

Thelma was all smiles, but I saw a sliver of hope stretch across her face. She'd lost the people that mattered most in her life. Her son, Charlie junior, was killed in Vietnam, and then she lost her husband. She must have felt so lonely sometimes.

The pain of losing my parents tore my heart to pieces, but each loss was independent of the other, and each relationship represented a distinctly different type of loss, and I couldn't begin to imagine how Thelma felt.

I hugged my right arm around her shoulder, partly to help guide her over the bumpy sidewalk, but also to offer the little comfort I could. "If we can, Thelma, we'll get a message to your husband and son, I promise."

She leaned her wig onto my shoulder, and the large bleached blonde bun hit my cheek. "Charlie and I talk every day. Even if I can't see him, I know he's with me. I feel him here still."

I smiled. Thelma was a trouper.

The Lye BBQ food truck sat parked next to the main entrance to section three of the lacrosse fields, and thankfully where Austin's game was. I strongly suggested Thelma pop a squat on one of the benches, but nope, she wanted to order her own food and be a part of the conversation with Jesse and Julia.

How could anyone say no to a little old woman in a Dolly Parton wig?

Jesse leaned out of the truck's serving area and smiled. "Well,

well, look who's come to try our barbecue." His belly jiggled when he talked, and from the way his eyes sparkled and the skin around them crinkled, I couldn't help but think he'd make a great old man. I imagined him sitting on an old rocker on the front porch of a home chewing on a piece of straw while his grandkids played in the yard.

Julia Lye shouted from behind him. "I don't care who's there. Just tell me if it's pork or chicken."

She was just such a lovely person.

"I'll take both," Thelma hollered back. "And no bread. I'm watching my figure."

Jesse laughed. "What can I get you?"

I really didn't want to sample any of the competitors' dishes. It wasn't against the competition rules, but as a judge, it seemed like poor etiquette, and given the fact that Lonna would very likely be writing an article slamming me, I didn't think it would help my case. "Just an iced tea for me."

"You sure?"

Julia stepped up to the window, pushing her husband aside with the bump of a hip. "You should try the pork. It's extra tender today."

"Thanks, but I just ate," I lied.

Thelma took out a ten dollar bill, but when she handed it to Jesse, he waved her off. "Senior discount is one hundred percent off."

Julia's displeasure at his freebie was obvious from her snarl. He ignored her and handed the plate full of chicken and pork BBQ to Thelma.

She examined it with a critical eye, leaned into me and whispered, "Looks a little on the dry side."

I chuckled.

"Hey Jesse, can we talk for a minute?" I glanced behind me. The line wasn't long, and I assumed his wife could handle it if he stepped away for a moment.

"Sure, gimme a sec." He wiped the top of his brow with a red cloth and disappeared into the back of the truck. A second later he was standing by my side. "What's up?"

With a mouth full of BBQ, chicken or pork, I wasn't sure, Thelma said, "We came to find out if you killed Bobby Pruitt so you could win the competition."

Jesse's eyes widened. "Uh, what?"

"Thelma, please." I shrugged at Jesse. "She doesn't mince her words. You've heard about his passing?"

He nodded. "Didn't much care for the man, but didn't wish him dead, either."

"Have the police talked to you?"

"No, ma'am, why?"

"They're talking to everyone that might have had a problem with Bobby."

He bounced on the tips of his toes. "I didn't have a problem with Bobby. I mean, we had a disagreement about business, but that's no reason to kill a man."

"Buddy Prakas ran his neighbor over with his horse and buggy for selling his crop at a penny less than his," Thelma said.

We both stared at her.

She waved her fork at us. "I wasn't there, of course, but that's the way the story goes."

"I don't have a horse and buggy."

"No, but you have a food truck, and that could do a doozy of damage."

I leaned my head back and sighed. "Thelma, that's not the way Bobby was killed."

She just shrugged and went back to eating her BBQ.

I didn't want to be dishonest with the man, and I wanted to get the truth out of him, too. "The morning Bobby was killed, I was at Hamilton House, so naturally, I'm a suspect. I didn't do it, and I'm determined to find out who did."

His body stiffened. "What's that got to do with me?"

"I'm just putting all of my cards on the table. I know there was animosity between the two of you. I saw it in the meeting. Where were you the next morning shortly before nine o'clock?"

He scratched his head. "You still a judge in the competition?"

I nodded.

His entire body stiffened, and the kindness he's generally worn on his face disappeared, replaced with bitterness and with a side of anger. "I don't really have to tell you anything, but if I don't, you're going to hold that against me in the competition then."

My stomach tied itself up into a knot, and not the kind that was easily undone. I instantly regretted my approach, and saw my volunteer position as a judge drive off after this year, if it even made it that far. "I would never do that. I'm simply trying to help my friend Delphina find out what happened to someone she cares deeply about, and clear my name. I have a son. I need to keep him safe."

He dipped his chin. "I know what it's like to lose someone we care about. I didn't kill the man. I was at the truck getting it prepped for the day. I'm there every morning bright and early."

"Where exactly is here?"

"We keep it at our house, of course, where we do most of our prepping."

"Can you explain what happened with the permit issue?"

"We got our permit for the truck, and we were doing great. People in town like options, you know? We're not trying to steal anybody's business, we're just trying to build our own. But Bobby, he didn't agree, and when he found out about us, he showed up here pitching a fit like we was out to destroy his place and all. He swore he'd close us down, and my wife, she's from Jersey, so she's not one to keep her opinions to herself, she told him where he could stick that threat, and we just ignored him." He stared off toward the lacrosse field. "We'd won the competition once before, and I think that was a big threat to Bobby, too.

Next thing we knew, there he was, pushing a cart right up next to the truck and selling his barbecue for half the price of ours. He didn't have a permit, so Julia reported him. We went to the city council meeting that following Monday to complain, and there he was, applying for an emergency retroactivated permit for the thing, and he got it."

I didn't know the Bobby Pruitt of late, but I remembered the one from high school, and he was definitely the kind of guy that did that sort of thing. "And after the meeting?"

He showed his palms and shrugged. "Nothing. He continued to park that cart here a few times a week, but we keep moving spots, and people, they caught on. We knew if they wanted our barbecue, they'd come. If they wanted his, they'd go to him. That deal at Hamilton House was his, not ours."

I wasn't exactly sure his wife felt the same way. "Okay. Thank you. I'd like to talk with Julia, too. Do you think that would be okay?"

"My wife was getting our daughter off to daycare. She does that every morning. We got a business to run, you know."

Thelma coughed. "I need to use the ladies' room again. That barbecue is going right through me, and quick, too."

"Duty calls. Thank you for talking with me."

"We didn't have nothing to do with that man's death, ma'am. We're just hardworking people looking to raise our daughter good and earn a good living."

Jack made it for the last quarter of the game. Austin flipped around and high fived him when Jack patted him on the back. I smiled on the inside. I wanted so much for Austin to reestablish his relationship with his father, but

I wanted his father to be worthy of it, and he hadn't been, at least not in Austin's eyes. Jack, however, was worthy of admiration, and that admiration was evident in my son's body language every time Jack was nearby.

It made my soul happy.

After scoring five out of the seven goals, the last two giving them the win, Austin stunk worse than a dog sprayed by a family of skunks. I did not want to let that boy in my car, but I couldn't let him walk home either. He'd stink up the rest of town for days, maybe longer.

I left Thelma on the first row of bleachers and walked over to my son. "Coach Jack said I owned the game."

Jack stood next to him, smiling. "I didn't say it that way. I said he rallied for the team."

"Same thing," Austin said. He picked up his water bottle and squirted water onto his face.

I cringed. The water would just exaggerate his rancid stench.

"He had a good game. You heading home?"

I nodded. "I've got Thelma with me. She wanted to come and watch."

He raised his brow, which I thought was for me, but when I heard the shrill of Lonna Appleton's Southern drawl behind me, I knew it wasn't.

CHAPTER 8

*L*onna narrowed her eyes at me. "What are you doing here?"

Jack ruffled my son's hair. "Lonna, this is Austin, Chantilly's son. She's here to watch him play."

A sheen of red heat crept up her face from her neck. "Oh, silly." She gave Jack a onearmed embrace and kissed him on the cheek. "I know that. I was talking to you."

In an alternative universe maybe, I thought.

"It's my team."

"Well, of course it is, sweetie, but don't you have that big murder to investigate and all?" She glared straight at me again. "Such a tragedy, don't you think, Chantilly? I sure hope the killer is found right quick."

I rolled my eyes.

"There was a murder? Here? Who?" Austin asked.

"Oh honey, your momma didn't tell you? Why it was—"

"Lonna." Jack's voice was deep and stern, like he was talking to a child.

I liked it.

She tilted her head, keeping her eyes locked on yours truly. "What?"

"What're you doing here?"

She wiggled the bag in her hand. "Why, I know you've been busy what with that murder investigation and all. I wanted to make sure you'd taken the time to eat, so I whipped something up for you and rushed over here to get it to you." She held the bag out for him. "It's an avocado, sprouts and egg salad sandwich, with olive oil mayo, of course, on multi-grain bread and a side of fruit." She squeezed his right bicep. "Got to keep my man healthy."

He smiled one of those kinds of smiles people gave a doctor when asked if it hurt while being poked and prodded in an area where they had pain. Nope doc, doesn't hurt a bit. He held the bag up, and for a second, I thought he was giving it back to her, but instead he said thank you.

She kissed his cheek again. "Anything for you, my love."

The whole while she stared at me. Lonna Appleton did not want me on her turf, and I knew the article she'd written would be her ammunition to make sure I wasn't.

I wasn't looking forward to reading it.

"Austin, would you mind walking Thelma over there to the car and getting her settled in the front seat, please? I'll be right there."

"But I always get shotgun."

"Yes, because there's never an older person with more life experience to take it from you, but tonight there is."

He wiggled his head like I'd just said the most ridiculous thing ever, but he did as I'd asked, and I considered that a win for momma.

"So Lonna, how's that article coming? You know, the one where you're planning to throw me under the bus for Bobby's murder?"

She swallowed hard. "I'm not...I...I'm reporting what my sources tell me, that's all."

Jack stood with his legs hip width apart and gripped his waist with his palms. "Did someone tell you they thought Chantilly killed Bobby?"

"Well, no, not...not exactly."

"What exactly did they tell you?"

"That they'd seen her at Hamilton House the morning he was killed."

"And that's enough evidence to convict her in the paper?"

"Well? I, uh...I...I just report what I'm told. That's my job."

I held up my hand. "Your job is to interview and ask questions and report the facts."

She stepped back and squinted her eyes at me. "And that's what I did."

"So then you're telling me the article mentions Maybelle Parker being there, arguing with Bobby, and being fired then, too?"

"Well, no, of course not. Maybelle Parker wouldn't hurt a flea."

"You can't stab a flea with a knife, Lonna."

"Whatever is that supposed to mean?"

"It means you didn't do your due diligence on that article, and you know it." She'd crossed the line, and I was angry. I was angry before, so why it came out then didn't make sense.

"Why, I can't believe you'd accuse me of such a thing. I'm a professional. I don't know what they taught you at that out of state college you went to, but I'm homegrown, and I learned from the best."

I secured a loose strand of my long red hair behind my ear and shook my head. "Deflecting never worked for you in high school, Lonna, and it's won't now, either."

Jack rubbed the top of his head. "I specifically asked you not to write about the suspects. What were you thinking?"

She winced. "I was thinking I needed to do my job."

"No, you weren't, that much I know. Pull the article."

"I can't. It's too late. It's already gone to print."

His head shifted back and forth, and then he pulled his cell phone out of his pocket. Before he dialed, he smiled at me. "I'm sorry about this. You going to be around in a bit?"

"I can wait here."

"No, go home. I'll come by in a bit." He whipped his head toward his girlfriend. "Go home, Lonna. We'll talk later. I need to fix this before it's too late. He marched away while tapping into his phone.

Goodness. Things had to be pretty bad for Lonna Appleton if I felt sorry for her, and I did.

I'd forgotten to turn the air to auto that morning, and Austin and I walked into a stuffy house. A hint of my mother's cranberry jam breezed by us as I closed the door behind us. "Did you smell that?"

Austin bolted past me toward the stairs. "Smell what?"

"Nothing."

"Can you make me something to eat, please? I'm getting in the shower."

I stood frozen and dumbfounded. My son had just willingly decided to take a shower. By himself. Without any threats of certain death from his mother.

Then again, when I got in the car to leave the field, I'd rolled up the windows to turn on the air conditioner, and Thelma asked if there was a dead opossum rotting behind her seat.

I'd replied with a simple, "Nope, that's my son."

She'd held her nose and said, "Heavens, that could kill an old person like me. I have a very sensitive nose."

"Dinner will be ready soon," I hollered to him.

I searched the freezer for one of my previously made chicken potpies and slid it into the oven when it hit the right temperature.

I set the small fourtop kitchen table my mother and I picked out in a big box furniture store a few years ago and stared at the wall.

I chose not to think about Lonna's article, and felt some sense of relief knowing Thelma's blog wouldn't accuse anyone else of the crime in my defense. On the way home, I'd quickly filled her in on Jack's desire to not have any names published and assured her there would be no need to do it at that point anyway. I prayed I was right, because I had no idea what Jack could do, if anything, to stop Lonna's article from printing, but I hoped for the best.

The floor creaked like they always did when someone walked down the hall. "It'll be ready in a bit," I said.

Austin didn't answer, and I didn't hear his unique, heavy footed walk toward the kitchen or the TV click on in the den.

"Austin?" I pushed the chair back from the table and walked into the hallway. The water beating down into the shower tub echoing from the bathroom.

He was still in the shower? But I'd just heard—I stopped my thought. I knew what I'd just heard, and it wasn't Austin. "Who's here?"

I got to the den just in time to see the last speckles of white as they disappeared. A piece of lined paper slipped from the coffee table to the floor. I picked it up to read it, but the words disappeared before my eyes. I walked in a circle, hoping she was still there. "Agnes? Please, Agnes, talk to me. I can't figure this out like this."

Austin leaned onto the French doors into the den. "Momma, you okay?"

I flipped around. "Oh, yes, sweetie, I'm fine. Just thought I heard something."

He didn't seem to care. "Dinner ready yet? I'm starving."

I checked my watch. "Three more minutes. Get yourself something to drink. I'll be in in a second."

He flipped around without a care in the world while I stood there holding a letter written in disappearing ink.

Austin spoke with a mouthful of chicken potpie. "Coach Jack's girlfriend is weird."

He was right, but there was a lesson hanging from his words, and I needed to teach it when I had the chance. "First impressions aren't always the best, sweetie, and you shouldn't be so quick to judge."

"I've met her before, and she was weird then, too."

Stop pitching me softballs, I thought. It was hard to be a mother and kind toward people that wanted to throw me under the bus at the same time. "You must have seen her when she had a lot on her mind or something."

"Maybe, because she acted like she didn't know me, and she does. Just the other day she sat next to me at practice and asked me all about us."

My fork stopped midway to my mouth. "She talked to you?"

"Yeah. Wanted to know if you and Dad would get back together and if you have a boyfriend." He cringed at the thought of one of those, I just wasn't sure which.

I kept my tone even and calm, and it wasn't easy. "What did you tell her?"

"I told her Dad's getting married, and you're too old for a boyfriend."

Both of those were stabs to my heart I hadn't expected, one more so than the other. "Your father's getting married?"

He looked up from his dinner. A small piece of carrot stuck to the side of his face, and I wiped it off with his napkin.

"He said he was gonna tell you."

I moved a chunk of chicken around on my plate. "Oh, well, he probably hasn't had a chance yet."

"He told me the day after we moved. He wants me to be his best man."

I swallowed a bite and it went down the wrong pipe. I coughed for a good thirty seconds straight.

We'd taught Austin how to perform the Heimlich Maneuver when he was younger, and he jumped from his seat immediately.

I held up my hand. "I'm okay," I said, coughing between words. "Give me a sec." I coughed a few more times, wiped my beginning to tear eyes, and finally spoke again. "That sounds great. Are you excited?"

He shrugged. "I mean, not really, I guess."

"Honey, look at me."

His eyes shifted upward, but he kept his head aimed toward his plate.

"It's okay. You're allowed to be happy for your dad, and you're allowed to look forward to sharing in his experiences. I'm fine." The funny thing was, I wasn't just saying that, either. I was fine. I wasn't thrilled to know Scott was marrying the woman he'd left me for, but I didn't exactly want him back, either.

I sensed how torn my son felt. A young boy didn't need that kind of pressure. It wasn't his responsibility to take on the burden of his parents' mistakes. "We made our mistakes, and we're both trying to rebuild our lives, but none of it is your responsibility. You have to do what you feel is right for you, and I'll support whatever that is." I stood and moved around the table and hugged my arms around his shoulders. I pressed my cheek onto his. "If your dad and I did anything right, it was creating you. You've got a good heart and a strong soul. Let those guide you."

"But I don't want you to be upset."

"First of all," I poured myself a glass of tea. "This isn't about me. This is about your father and his special day. Second of all, I will never be upset with you for wanting to support your father. I expect that from you."

"So, you mean you'd be disappointed if I didn't do it?"

I wouldn't go that far, but I knew where he was going. He wanted my approval. "I think you should do it. I think in the long term, you'll be happy you did."

His mouth twitched, and I knew he wanted to smile, but wasn't sure if he should. I chose to change the subject. "But I have a bone to pick with you."

He sighed. "I hate when you pick at my bones."

I smirked. "Too bad. I made those bones in my body. I can pick at them all I want."

"Fine."

"How am I too old to have a boyfriend?"

He laughed. "Boyfriends are for girls my age, Momma. You're old. You should have a man friend."

"Semantics, Austin, semantics."

"What're those?"

I ruffled his hair and it reminded me of when Jack had done it earlier and also that I hadn't yet heard from him. "Don't you have homework?"

"A little."

"I'll clean up. Go get it started. It's getting late."

"Yes, ma'am."

I dug my phone out of my purse and saw I had a voicemail from Delphina. I played it back.

"Sweetie, it's Del. Hello. Are you there? Listen, call me. I talked to the cooks, and I wanted to fill you in. Okay? Bye. Stupid machine."

I laughed. Del couldn't grasp that voicemail wasn't like an

answering machine. I couldn't just pick up in the middle of the message. I did call her back, and she answered.

"That Rashid Patel was at Hamilton House that morning."

"What? He was?"

"Yup. Both cooks said he came in looking for Bobby, and they sent him upstairs just like you."

"How long was he there?"

"Don't know. They didn't see him leave."

"He could have had plenty of time to kill Bobby even if he was there five minutes before I was."

"You've seen Rashid. The man's a stick. Can't weigh more than my old dog, Red, and he wasn't even a hundred and ten pounds. I don't think he could kill Bobby."

"He could if Bobby wasn't expecting it."

"Bobby's a confrontational guy, or he was anyway. He wouldn't let that kid in his office in the first place."

That could have been true, but someone was there, and they killed him. "Maybe Bobby didn't let him into the office. Maybe the killer was already there."

"How's that?"

My phone beeped and Jack's contact information flashed on my screen. "Del, that's Jack on the other line, and I've got to talk to him. I'll come by first thing tomorrow, okay?"

"Hanging up on me for that detective, are ya? Em hmm." She hung up her landline, and I laughed.

I answered Jack's call. "Hey."

"Hey. I wanted to apologize for Lonna's behavior earlier."

"Please. It's nothing she hasn't done to me in the past. Don't worry about it."

"I had a talk with her, and I don't think she'll behave like that again."

"Wanna bet?"

"Excuse me?"

"Nothing. Just thinking out loud. Did you find out anything about the article?"

"Chip, the guy that runs the paper is a good friend. You probably remember him from school."

"I do."

"He pulled it. I let him know what's going on and why I don't want any potential suspects named yet."

I breathed a sigh of relief even though he'd called me a potential suspect. "Thank you so much."

"Not a problem."

"You know I didn't do it though, don't you? I could never do something like that."

"I don't think you did, but I have to ask the questions and check all the boxes."

I understood that. "Have you talked to Julia and Jesse Lye or Rashid Patel?"

"I have them on my list. We don't have a large department, and I've got a few people handling other things at the moment, so it's pretty much just me."

"I ran into Julia and Jesse at the lacrosse park tonight."

"They do have their food truck there."

"Yes, and they were both very upset the other day about Bobby having his cart there. Bobby argued with them. I told you that, right?"

"Yes, ma'am."

Ew. I understood what Angela Panther said. I didn't like being called ma'am by someone my age. It hadn't occurred to me before, but it stood out like a sore thumb when Jack said it. "When I spoke to them this evening, Jesse didn't really have an alibi. He said he was prepping his truck at his house and that his wife took their daughter to daycare."

"Okay."

"And I don't know what happened, but Delphina just said Rashid Patel, another one of the contestants in the competition, was at Hamilton House the morning Bobby was killed."

"Yes, I know."

"You knew? Why didn't you tell me?"

"You're not part of the investigation."

Ego deflated. "No, but that doesn't matter. If I'm a possible suspect, I have a right to know the other suspects, don't I?"

"You don't actually have rights to know what's going on. The department determines what's appropriate for the public to know. That's how these things work."

"I'm sorry. I've never been accused of murder, so I wouldn't know." There was a whole lot of attitude in my tone when I blurted out that immature statement.

"In an active investigation a law enforcement officer doesn't typically share key points with anyone potentially involved in the case. Call it poor business practice."

"I get it." And I did. I just didn't like being a possible suspect. "The cooks told Del they talked to Rashid, but they didn't see him leave. Don't you think that's odd?"

"Not impossible. He naturally went into the kitchen looking for Bobby. They directed him upstairs, and when he finished his business, he left through the front door. Maybe he didn't feel the need to say goodbye to the staff."

"It's possible, I guess. Can you at least tell me what time he got there?"

"Said shortly before nine."

"I left the museum just before nine. I saw Maybelle and chatted with her for all of two minutes maybe and then went straight to the restaurant. Wouldn't I have seen Rashid?"

"He probably drove."

"But if he was there for even just five minutes, it's likely I would have at least run into his car leaving or something, right?"

He was silent for a moment. "Could be."

"What did he go there for?"

"Chantilly, listen. I appreciate what you're doing here, but this is a police investigation, and I really have to keep it private."

"Yes, I know. I'm sorry. I appreciate you talking to Chip for me."

"How's your head?"

"It's better, thank you for asking."

"Not planning to perform any more séances now, are you?"

"Not anytime in the future, no."

"Good. The last thing this town needs is someone telling them these old ghost stories are true."

CHAPTER 9

"*H*e did not." Delphina slid a sliced biscuit onto my plate and handed it to me across the counter. "I was there. I saw it with my own eyes. I know there's ghosts in this town."

"You haven't seen Agnes. You've seen me seeing Agnes. That's something entirely different."

She sat at my table with me. "Well, that boy wouldn't know a ghost if it tossed a white sheet over its head and sat at his table for supper."

I laughed. "You're probably right, but a lot of people don't believe in them. I wasn't sure I did before now, either."

"I've seen a ghost before," Thelma said.

Del wiggled her head like a frustrated mother. "Yeah? When?"

"When Charlie Junior died, I knew. I knew before they came to tell us. I saw him in my dream. He told me he was okay, and that I shouldn't worry. He said Heaven was pretty, but I had a long time before I got there, and I needed to be strong."

Del's face softened. "How come you never told me that?"

"You never asked."

From what I recalled, Charlie was missing in action for over two months before they found him. Thelma hadn't heard from him, but that wasn't unusual for families with loved ones in the heat of the battle. "How long before the men came to your house after you had the dream?"

"Oh heavens, I don't recall, but at least several weeks. I told Big Charlie, and we both knew it was him. In our hearts, we knew."

"I'm so sorry," I said.

Thelma smiled and adjusted her wig. "It's okay. He's okay, and I know that. I'll see him again. Big Charlie, too."

Del centered Thelma's lopsided wig. "I like the blue ribbon. It goes nicely with your yellow dress."

"I was reminded of Buster, so I decided to wear yellow in his honor."

I shifted in my seat and stared out the café door.

"What's wrong?" Thelma asked.

I flipped back around. "Nothing, I just wanted to make sure lightning didn't strike the café." I winked, and she laughed.

Del pursed her lips. "Oh, shut it. I got a heart."

Thelma leaned in and whispered, "It might be turning black, but it's still got a little touch of red to it."

Del grunted and walked behind the counter, mumbling what I suspected was something unkind and inappropriate the entire way.

"Jack said he already spoke to Rashid Patel," I said upon her return with the coffee pot.

"Yeah, Rashid said that. I would have told you, but you hung up too quick."

"You hung—never mind. Did he happen to tell you why he went there?"

"Something about wanting to make amends with Bobby. Said he wanted to forgive and forget."

How convenient, I thought. "Did he talk to him?"

She nodded. "Said Bobby was okay with it, too."

"Does that strike you as strange?"

"What? Bobby forgiving someone?"

I nodded.

"Do deer eat gardens?"

Thelma sipped her coffee and said, "Actually, yes, they do, but my neighbor Mr. Hamby said there's stuff at the hardware store to stop them. When I read the label, it said it had poison in it, so I didn't buy it."

"Why not?" Del asked.

"Because I didn't want to poison myself, silly. What do you think?"

Del dipped her head back and pressed her hands together to pray. "Dear God, bless her heart. I don't know how she's survived all these years."

"I walk every day and don't drink or smoke."

Del threw her hands up in the air. "I wasn't talking to you. I was praying for patience to God."

I stopped myself from laughing. "Anyway, I know I've said it before, but I didn't really know Bobby all that well, except for high school, of course, but even then, he wasn't the nicest guy. To think he'd suddenly change his tune overnight like that is kind of hard to believe."

"Well, I knew Bobby real good, and once he's mad, he stays mad. No way he made amends with Rashid."

"Then why would he lie?" Thelma asked.

"Because he killed him, that's why," Del said, and rather loudly, too.

"Del."

She stared at me. "What?"

"You don't want to scare your customers away, do you?"

She waved her hand. "I do that every day."

"We don't want to publicize who we think might have killed Bobby."

She gasped. "Oh, yeah. You're right. Sorry about that."

"In speaking with Jesse and Julia—well, Jesse really—I don't get the feeling he did it. He was genuinely surprised I could have been asking if he had. But he made it pretty clear, without actually saying it, that he didn't want me talking to his wife."

"Probably just wanted to protect her," Thelma said. "My Charlie used to do that all the time. Never even let me answer the doorbell when those religious people came by. Said he didn't want me to invite them in, but I knew it was his way of protecting me."

"Nah, he just didn't want them in his house," Del said.

I rolled my eyes. "Anyway, Julia is a hot one, and I'm a little wary of her."

"What do you mean?"

"I can't explain it. She's obviously got a temper, and when we got there last night, she was blatantly rude."

Delphina broke off a chunk of my biscuit and stuffed it into her mouth. "Killers can be feisty."

"She does have a lot to lose."

Thelma took part of the biscuit, also. I was grateful it was free, since I'd yet to take a bite. "Like what?" she asked.

"Bobby's cart threatened their business, their livelihood, and they have a child. It's not easy nowadays, and maybe she snapped."

"But nobody saw her at Bobby's that morning."

"Doesn't mean she wasn't there." Del folded a paper napkin into a square and flattened it with the palm of her hand. "So, we've got one hot tempered momma with everything to lose, and a forgiving business owner who can't tell time? Doesn't sound like much."

"And a fired employee, and yours truly."

"You didn't kill Bobby."

"And the husband. And if you watch TV, it's always the husband," Thelma said.

"I don't think it is in this kind of scenario, Thelma," I said.

"Don't matter, the pickin's are slim, that's for sure, and I got to get lunch started." Delphina stood, but before she headed back into the kitchen, she said, "I think you need to have another meeting with Agnes. Somehow that knife got into the office and stuck in Bobby's back, and my guess is she knows what happened."

———

Olivia handled the second tour of the day, a group of seniors from a neighboring town, while I finished a few tasks on the competition's to do list.

We'd considered canceling the event entirely, but the town looked forward to it, so instead, we decided to do it in Bobby's honor. That meant among other things, adding some additional posters, letting the Mayor know to change his opening speech, and reconfiguring the contestants' booth spaces.

Once I'd finished that, I sat down to once again rewrite the information for Hamilton House. I wanted to edit Agnes's story as well as add something to honor Bobby.

As I tapped onto my keyboard, I heard Olivia chatting with the seniors downstairs. She handled the tours so well, and it was a joy to listen to her.

I glanced up at my door, and a chunky old woman with gray hair in tight curls smiled at me. "I always wanted to come here. I think the town is quite charming."

I smiled back at her. "Thank you, we think it's a wonderful place to live. I'm glad you're here. Are you enjoying the tour?"

"Oh, yeah. I was here the other day, but I noticed you added a new exhibit in the main room. There sure is a lotta history in this place."

I hadn't recalled seeing her the other day. "Oh, yes. We change it up often. You'll have to come back again soon."

"Oh, I will," she said, and then she turned around and left.

I reworded the rest of the changes for Hamilton House, printed it out, and read it out loud. Once I finished, I leaned back in my chair and sighed. This will never fly with City Council, I thought. I wanted it to, but without any basis for the information, it just wouldn't. How could I tell them all I'd seen Agnes Hamilton's ghost and she'd showed me her murder, not her suicide? And even if they did believe I saw anything, who's to say Agnes isn't just trying to save her reputation by making it up? I wondered if I should wait to redo it, given the fact that Bobby's murder hadn't been solved. I would likely have to rewrite it then again, anyway.

Glass shattered in the other room, and a loud screeching scream echoed down the hall. I jumped out of my seat and rushed to the bedroom we used for storage.

An old Tiffany style lamp we'd stored in there recently lay on the ground, the glass shade a puzzle of multicolored pieces scattered on the hardwoods.

Olivia stormed in, breathless from running up the stairs. "Oh Lord, did you fall again?"

"No, I'm fine. The lamp, it must have fallen. I heard the crash and came running."

"Oh, Miss Chantilly, your scream scared the living daylights out of me."

"It wasn't me. I...Is everyone okay downstairs? What about the old woman that came up here?" It was possible she snuck into the room and accidentally knocked over the lamp.

Olivia tilted her head. "What little old lady?"

"The one with the tightly curled gray hair. She's about this high." I held my hand, palm facing the ground, to my chest. "Wearing a blue sweater and tan pants?"

"Miss Chantilly, there's no women in this tour. It's the senior men's club today."

"What? No, she was just up here."

She shrugged. "Either your concussion's getting worse, or you're seeing the dead everywhere now." She walked out the door. "I need to get back to the old men before one of them starts looking for the booze he thinks is hidden downstairs. I keep telling him there isn't any, but the little stinker doesn't believe me."

I sulked back to my office, confused and frustrated. Before I got there, I glanced down the elaborate, elegant staircase at the group of men waiting for Olivia. Nope, not one single woman with tightly curled gray hair in the group.

Could she have been a spirit? Did they really just show up and chat with people like that? I fell into my chair and sighed. "How will I know the difference?"

I searched through my previous calls from the night before and clicked on the number for Angela Panther. I hit call and it rang twice before she picked up.

"Hey, Chantilly, I wondered how long it would take for you to call me."

"I'm sorry, is this a bad time?"

"Not in the least. I'm just having a discussion with my mom. Hey, maybe you can clear something up for us. You're from the South, right?"

"Yes, but I—"

"Okay, which do you prefer, George Strait or Blake Shelton?"

"I, uh…"

"Neither of us will hold it against you. I promise."

"Well, I do like Blake, I think he's really talented."

"I knew it." The phone made a static like sound. "See, Ma? New country is good, too."

Her mother said, "George is the king of country. Nobody can top him."

"She does have a point," I said.

"You heard my mother?"

"Yes, why?"

"My mother's been dead for over ten years."

I dropped the phone in my lap.

"Chantilly? Hello?"

I picked it up, stared at it, and then stared at the chunky old woman with tight gray curls waving at me in the hallway. She smiled, winked, and then kind of shimmered away right before my eyes, leaving little sparkles of light fading away behind her.

"I'm here. I'm here. I...does your mom have tightly curled gray hair? And is she short?" I whispered, "Maybe a little on the heavy side?"

"Good grief. Yes, that's her." Angela's voice muffled. "Ma, I told you not to play around with Chantilly. Geez."

"What? A gal can't have a little fun now and then? I just wanted to make sure she wasn't messin' with my daughter, is all. What's she gonna do, sue me?"

Oh my gosh, I really could see, talk, hear...oh my gosh. My hands shook, and I needed to sit. I was dizzy. The problem was, I was sitting.

"Ma, enough. You can't do that, and you know it. Now apologize to Chantilly. You probably just gave her a heart attack."

"Ah Madone, she didn't even know I'm dead."

The old lady peeked into my office again, her head only a foot above the doorknob. "Sorry. I didn't mean to upset you." And then she was gone, just like that.

"She, uh...she just...she just apologized."

Angela sighed. "Good."

My head hurt. "Help me." My voice shook, but it almost came out comical.

"You'll adjust, I promise. Your gift is pretty strong though. It'll be interesting if you ever figure out how you got it."

"You mean I might not? Does that mean I'll always have it?"

"It's possible. I can't say for sure either way.

I closed my eyes. "I think I need a glass of wine, but I don't drink."

"I go for cupcakes and Snickers bars. They help. So does coffee, and lots of it."

I laughed, and once I started, I couldn't stop. I laughed so hard, it ended up silent, and tears streamed down my face. "I'm... I'm sorry."

"Don't sweat it. If you can laugh, you are farther along in accepting this than I was, so good for you."

"How long did it take you?"

"A few years."

"Seriously?"

"I'm a stubborn Italian from Chicago, it runs in my blood. So, is the little gray haired woman the reason you called?"

"Yes, and no, but you can tell her that lamp was expensive."

Angela relayed the message to her mother.

"That wasn't me. That was the chick in the wedding gown. She's one ticked off spirit, let me tell you."

"Oh boy. She said—"

"I heard. It's Agnes, and I think I know why she's upset."

"Why?"

I explained my job, what I needed to do for Hamilton House's information, and what I'd written. "I'm trying to do what I can to help her, like you said. The problem is, no one here is going to accept that as fact just because I wrote it, and I'm sure not going to say her ghost told me."

"May I make a suggestion?"

"Yes, please do."

"Don't do anything, at least not yet."

"I don't understand."

"Okay, for starters, you don't want her to leave, not yet anyway."

"But isn't that my goal?"

"Yes, of course, at least eventually. She can help you with the other murder though, so you need her to stick around."

"That's true."

"It's not the only reason. You should always consider the unintended consequences for your actions. Believe me, that was a hard lesson for me to learn, and I'd rather not see anyone else struggle through it."

Considering I'd just moved back to town, taken a new job, and was now a possible murder suspect, Angela made sense. I also needed to consider Austin and his life. "So what do I do?"

"Wait it out. She might have more to say soon, or give you something you need for the other murder."

"I guess, but it would be much easier if she just came out and said it. I saw your mother clear as day, and we had a conversation. Why can't they all do that?"

"Because the universe likes to mess with our heads."

She tossed out a few other thoughts, all pertaining to the knife because we knew it was the thing that connected the two murders. We just didn't know what Agnes was trying to tell me.

Angela Panther forced me to think through the events, to think about different possibilities. I might have been a newbie with respect to spirits, but I was a puzzle solver. "I know what you're doing." I laughed. "I have a kid. I'm an expert at this kind of thing."

She laughed, too. "Then think it through, and when you figure it out, call me. I have some theories, but I think you need to come up with them first." She paused for a moment and said, "This is a lot of fun, helping you. It's taking me away from my current situation, so I appreciate it."

"Are you working another case for the police?"

"No. I'm being dragged into something I'd rather not be dragged into, and I'm heading to Chicago because of it."

"Oh, I'm sorry."

"Things happen."

We talked further, said we'd talk again soon, and after we

hung up I thought about what she'd said. Before I could come to any conclusions though, I needed to know if the knife was from the restaurant. I had to assume it was, at least based on convenience, unless of course the killer had planned to kill Bobby before coming. If that was the case, then the knife could be from anywhere. First things first. Find out about the knife and hope it led me to the killer.

I dialed Jack's cell.

"Chantilly, I was just thinking about you."

I wasn't sure how to respond to that, so I didn't. "May I ask a question about the investigation?"

"Didn't we recently have a conversation about this?"

"Yes, I know, but I'm trying to work through a few things, and just this one teeny little bit of information will help me."

"I can't guarantee I can answer, but go ahead."

Gosh, he was a stickler for the rules. "Was the knife from the restaurant?"

"Why do you ask?"

Because the spirit of Agnes Hamilton isn't making that clear to me, and I want to figure out which death it belongs to. No, I didn't say that. I wanted Jack to take me seriously. "I'm curious since there are a few people on my suspect list that would have access to knives."

"Your suspect list?"

Darn it. "You know what I mean. If I'm a potential suspect, I need to figure out who else is, and I'm trying to get all my ducks in a row."

"Maybe you should hire an attorney to straighten your ducks?"

My heart raced. "Do I need an attorney?"

"No, Chantilly, at this point you do not. However, you establishing a suspect list sounds an awful lot like you're trying to investigate this on your own, and I wish you wouldn't. That could cause my real investigation serious problems."

"I'm not investigating. I'm just...I just...ugh. Can you please tell me?"

He sighed heavily. "Yes, the weapon matched knives from Hamilton House, but they're common and could be owned by anyone that has their own restaurant business."

"So anyone in the restaurant could have had access to one there, or anyone in that kind of business could, too?"

"Yes, ma'am."

"Thank you."

"Is that all?"

"Did you know that Rashid Patel wanted to buy and then rent Bobby's place?"

"Where'd you hear that?"

"From him. He said he couldn't actually afford to purchase it, but since he'd heard Bobby was thinking about selling it, he wanted to know if he could lease it now."

"He wants to lease the space? Is it going up for lease?"

"Yes, and I don't know, but Delphina said there was no way Bobby would ever consider selling, and when we pressed him for information, we couldn't get much more out of him."

"I'll check into it."

"That's a good idea. Let me know what you find out."

He muttered something about women being the death of him and we disconnected. I chuckled at that.

The suspect list continued to grow, and any success I thought I'd made, which wasn't all that much, flew right out the window. Who could I confirm would have access to the knife? I counted the number of people on my hands, and there were several. I took it a step further. Who had access to the knife as well as a motive? Other than myself, four people. When I added opportunity, that list stayed the same.

I didn't count the two cooks in the kitchen when I got there. I probably should have, but my gut told me it was one of three people, and neither of them were on that list.

CHAPTER 10

I jumped in my car and drove over to Rashid Patel's restaurant. He'd chosen the perfect location for access on and off the interstate, but I understood his concern about the size of the place. What I didn't understand was how he'd thought he could get a hold of Bobby's.

Located in a small strip mall on the edge of town, his restaurant housed the prime corner unit, but it was tiny. The sign on the door was flipped to closed, but lights were on, and I knew he'd be getting ready for lunch, so I knocked.

Rashid peeked out from the kitchen, waved and strolled over. He didn't act like a man that had just committed murder, but I doubted I'd recognize someone that had.

"Hello, Miss Adair. What can I do for you?" His eyes shifted back and forth as he checked the parking lot.

"I just wanted to ask you a few quick questions."

He nodded. "Come in. Come in. Is it in regard to the competition?"

"No, it's not."

"Yes, yes. I am just preparing another batch of my secret

recipe barbecue. Would you like a sample? It's quite good this morning."

"Oh, no thank you, I had breakfast, and I'm stuffed, but I appreciate it."

"Well, come. Sit. Perhaps you would like tea or coffee or perhaps a traditional Indian drink? I can offer you chaach or aam panna. They are quite tasteful."

"No, I'm fine. This shouldn't take long."

He stood there, just nodding and staring at me. Finally, he said, "Okay."

I stayed standing. Looking up at the slender man from a seat didn't seem like the right way to go about asking him my questions. "I understand you went to see Bobby Pruitt the morning he died?"

He blinked and nodded. "Yes, yes. I wanted to make amends. I do not like discord or trepidation in my life. I try hard to cleanse it. It is very freeing."

"Yes, I imagine it is. What made you decide to do that?" I scanned the tables, and I noticed the utensils and napkins were in a small serving station in the corner near the kitchen. I needed to get a look at one of the knives. If they at least had a similar look to what I'd seen sticking out of Bobby's back, I'd have to keep Rashid on the list. If they didn't, I'd keep him on the list, but he'd be on the bottom of it.

"I did not want to enter the competition with an angry mind. I wanted to stream positivity in, and to do that, I needed to express my apologies and forgive, even if Mr. Pruitt could not forgive me."

I coughed. "You know, on second thought, my throat is a little dry. I'd love some water if you don't mind."

"Yes, yes. I can do that for you. One moment, please." He walked back to the kitchen.

When he was out of eyesight, I scurried over to the serving station, plucked a knife from the utensil cups and examined it quickly. I'd need to somehow compare it to the knives at Bobby's, so I stashed it in my purse. Great. Clearing myself from a murder suspect list made me a thief.

He returned from the kitchen and handed me a glass of water without ice. I sipped it because I didn't want to be a hypocrite and a liar. "Thank you."

"You were asking?"

"Oh, yeah. Was Bobby willing to forgive?"

"Oh, yes. He was quite happy. We discussed it briefly, and made our amends, and then I was on my way."

"How long were you there?"

"I was there five minutes."

"Wow, that's pretty exact."

He pointed to his temple. "I have a good sense of these things."

Or else you're a liar, I thought. "Okay, well, thank you. I appreciate it. I'm looking forward to the competition."

"I am quite excited. I have addressed some issues with my family recipe, and I have made improvements. It will be ready, and it will be the best there. I will win."

He might be a winner, but he was definitely a liar. There was no way Bobby Pruitt made any kind of amends with Rashid Patel.

———

My Fitbit said it was coming up on ten o'clock, so I assumed Jesse Lye was at home prepping his food truck. I did a quick search online to find his address, and thankfully the food truck popped up to what I suspected was his home. He wasn't far from where I was, so I headed over there, hoping I could sneak a look at his knife collection.

It was Julia prepping the food truck though, not Jesse. She crouched down on the back side of it, scrubbing the door forcefully. I walked up and tensed immediately when I saw her.

"What do you want now?" she asked. Her snarl wavered, and she actually forced a pitiful half smile and froze it onto her face. "I'm sorry. Rough few days. The police just left."

"I know things are tense with the competition and all, but I'm hoping you can tell me what happened with y'all, in your own words."

"Why? Jesse already told you everything, and I really don't think it's any of your business."

"We both had some kind of confrontation with Bobby. I'm just trying to piece everything together so we can all get on with our lives."

"I think I'll leave the investigation to the cops, not some small town divorcée looking to add a little excitement to her life."

Ouch. That wasn't necessary.

She scrubbed the door in one spot for so long I thought the paint would come off. She tossed the brush into the bucket beside her. "I can tell you this though, Bobby? He'd never make it in Jersey, I know that much. People there don't put up with jerks like him."

I nodded. "Are you still planning to attend the competition?"

She stood and swiped the back of her hand across her forehead. "Why wouldn't we? It's great for business, and God knows we need that after the crap that tyrant put us through."

"Do you prepare the food in your house?"

She nodded. "Listen, I have a lot to do. Jess took our daughter to daycare today for a change, and I'd like to get some stuff done before he's back. So, if you're done questioning me…"

"Just one more thing. What's your favorite knife brand?"

Her face turned red. "I'd like you to leave now." She opened the back of the truck and stepped inside.

———

I knew where Maybelle Parker lived, and headed that direction. It wasn't far from Julia and Jesse Lye's place. My mother would have said to take the gravel road to the big farm with the metal fence, turn right there, and then go through the red light and it's the sixth house on the left, just past the fire hydrant. Which is where it was, and hearing my mom's voice in my head gave me comfort.

Maybelle greeted me at the door, her nose red and eyes puffy, like she'd been crying. "Oh, Chantilly, can you believe it? It's just terrible, isn't it? Poor Bobby."

Funny, I thought. Just recently she'd acted like she wanted the man dead herself. Could she be behaving according to a plan to seem innocent? Maybe Maybelle Parker wasn't as nice as everyone thought after all? "It's terrible. No one should ever die under circumstances like that."

"At least he's with his momma now." We'd been standing at her door, and she asked me in. "What's brought you here today?"

"I'm just checking with all of the contestants, to make sure everyone is still interested in the competition, and considering what happened, I thought I'd come talk to you personally, check and see if you're okay."

"Why, of course, we are. Like the signs say, we're doing this for Bobby. I wouldn't have it any other way. In fact, I'm thinking of using his recipe, you know, in honor of him."

"I'm not sure that's a good idea."

I followed her into the kitchen, where she had me sit at a

twotop Formica table as she poured herself a coffee. "Would you like one?"

"Sure." I searched the counters for knives.

"I think Bobby would appreciate it. You know, we used to fight all the time, it wasn't anything, fighting with him that day. He just knew how to drive people crazy, that's all."

I nodded. "Have you decided what you're going to do for a restaurant?"

"I've got something in the works. A partner and I have been working on something kind of on the downlow and all, and I think now it might actually happen."

"Oh, that must be exciting. What's going on?"

Her doorbell rang. "Give me a second. I've been waiting for a delivery."

She walked out, and I immediately rushed to the counter and gave each drawer a quick look. I found the knives in the larger drawer and grabbed one. I hurried back to my seat and put it in the back pocket of my purse. I needed to remind myself which knife I'd stashed where, so I quickly typed out a note on my phone.

She came in carrying a large box as I finished and heaved it onto her counter. "Woohee, that was heavy."

"That's a big box. I could have helped with it."

She wiped her hands on her jeans. "It's fine. I knew it would be heavy. I ordered some samples for my new place, you know, dishes and silverware. I want something a little more farmhouse like, a little more modern than what I'm used to. Would you like to see?"

"Sure."

She opened the box on the counter and held up a place setting for one, including a spoon and fork, "I'm thinking of something like this. What do you think?"

"I like the blue and white lines. It's very simple, but fresh."

She reached into the box again, and had to step on her tiptoes that time. "I love these knives. They're lovely."

The knives were the same as the one I'd just taken from her drawer.

"Yes, lovely."

"You've seen them before, I'm sure. They're like the ones at Hamilton House."

"Oh, really? I hadn't noticed."

She stared at me, twirling a knife in her hand. "Yes, the knives he puts on the tables. He's had them for years. I thought it would be nice to freshen up the look though, get some new ones."

"Do you mean for Bobby's house?"

She flinched. "Oh, no. For my place."

Maybelle Parker was lying. "I wonder what's going to happen to Hamilton House now that Bobby's gone?"

"I'm sure the property will be sold."

"I'll have to ask Delphina if Bobby had a will."

She narrowed her eyes at me. "Why would he have a will?"

I shrugged. "He was my age, and I do. You never know what's going to happen. Everyone should have one."

"So, if he left his business to someone, they could run it there?"

I nodded. "Or he could have left the building to someone, and they can do whatever they want with it, as long as it's within the historical society's regulations."

She raised an eyebrow. "I hadn't thought about that."

"Why would you?"

She shook her head. "Oh, nothing. I just meant now. I hadn't considered that given the circumstances. Anyway, I've got some things to get done before I meet with the bank again. I'm moving forward with my life like I said." She took my cup from her Formica table and placed it in the sink. "I hate to rush you out like this though. We should get together again soon. After the competition, maybe?"

I stood and smiled. "Sure."

As I walked to my car, I sent Olivia a text and asked her to check on the competition rules for using recipes not originally entered into the competition.

"Hey, Miss Chantilly." Olivia met me at the front door to the historical society and blocked the entrance with her body.

"Sure, can I have a second to get inside though, please?"

She moved aside and let me in. "Oh, bless my heart. I'm sorry. I wasn't thinking."

I laughed. "It's okay, sweetie."

"I've been doing what you asked, and I found out something important about Mr. Dilts."

I walked back to the kitchen and poured myself a glass of Olivia's employee only sweet tea. When I took a sip, I understood why she didn't want to share it with the public. It tasted like golden sunshine and fresh honey. "This is amazing, Olivia."

She blushed. "Thank you."

I crooked my finger. "Come on up. We can chat while I'm getting my stuff out."

She followed me upstairs, and I unpacked my bag as we talked.

"Did you know Mr. Dilts died in jail?"

She'd caught me off guard, and I stopped mid bagemptying. "No way."

"Yes, well, after he left Castleberry, seems he ran off with that other woman to Kentucky, married her, and seven years later she was found dead in their home."

"Let me guess, she was hanged."

She nodded. "Judge sent him to jail, where he hanged himself a few weeks later."

"That doesn't sound like coincidence."

"It sure doesn't."

"Was there a letter?"

"Yes, ma'am. It was written in his wife's handwriting, but it was shaky, and given the other evidence, the judge felt she'd been coerced to write it. That and the fact that his neighbor walked in to see her hanging there, swinging from the rafter, and Josiah Dilts was having a drink in the parlor, staring at her. Can you imagine?"

"No, I can't, but maybe he was in shock?"

"But these make it sound like she knew it was coming."

She handed me two documents, both printed from images of diary pages.

I fear for my life. My husband is not the man I thought he was. I worry I have not long to live, and I fear his fiancée suffered a terrible fate, at his hand, too. Oh, how I wish I had known.

"Wow. That's a big sign right there."

"It most certainly is."

"Can you dig up anything else on the trial or something?"

"I've been in touch with the Bardwell Historical Society, and they're emailing me some documents. He was a big deal there for some time, and from what I understand, he wasn't well liked either." She showed me three additional documents detailing how not nice Mr. Josiah Dilts actually was.

Josiah Dilts' wife died in a similar situation as Agnes Hamilton, and that made it a lot easier for me to fight for her reputation in Castleberry. Angela Panther was right. Waiting it out was the way to go. "This is perfect, thank you, Olivia."

"Yes, ma'am." She left my office. "I've got a tour coming in in a bit, so I'm going to prepare for that," she said as she walked out.

I looked up toward the ceiling. "I'm doing my best," I said to Agnes. I just hoped she was there to hear me.

CHAPTER 11

I headed straight to Delphina's, pulled into her back lot, and entered through her back entrance. "Look." I carefully removed each knife from my purse and laid them on her desk. "Any of these look familiar?"

They were both the same brand and style.

"Why you got Bobby's knives in your purse? I'm starting to worry about you."

"That's exactly what I thought. I just needed you're confirmation to be sure."

"What for?"

"They're not Bobby's. One's from Rashid's restaurant and the other is Maybelle Parker's. And I couldn't get one from Jesse and Julia. She wouldn't let me out of her sight."

"We all get knives from the same supply company. Most people do." She walked over to her counter and pulled a knife out of the drawer. "See?"

"Oh." I examined the knives thoroughly. Look." I held up Rashid's knife. Its blade didn't have any small rust spots and it wasn't loose in the handle. My knives were all well used, and old, and many of them had tiny rust spots dotted on the metal. A few were on their last days, loose in my grip from a worn handle. I pointed that all out to Del.

"Yeah, so?"

"Now, look at Maybelle's knife. I wiggled the blade and it moved inside the handle. "That's an older knife."

"What are you getting at?"

"Did Bobby recently purchase his knives?"

She laughed. "You kidding? Bobby didn't spend a dime unless he had to. But I still don't see what you're getting at."

"Do you know where he keeps the utensils? Is there a station for them in the dining room somewhere?"

"Oh, heavens, no. It's a nice establishment, not some poorly run franchise. He keeps that stuff in back." She shook her head. "Don't matter anyway. That knife that went flying through the dining room, it wasn't a serving knife. It was a carving knife."

"How do you know?" It looked like a regular steak knife to me, but I was by no means a cook.

"'Cause I got the same ones, remember?" She pulled another knife out of her drawer. "This here's a carving knife. This particular brand's looks just like a steak knife, but the blade is sharper. They can easily pass as steak knives, and are cheaper than their competition, so I know for a fact Bobby bought them. Saved himself some money, too because they're cheaper than the actual steak knives if you buy them in bulk."

I barely saw the difference, but that made sense. "So the person either brought it, or they got it at Bobby's, and if so, they had to go into the kitchen and get it since the dining room wasn't set, which meant it's possible one of the two cooks there might remember seeing something."

"Only if they weren't the one that killed him, and if it wouldn't be unusual for the killer to have a knife in their hand."

"Maybelle."

"I don't think I can see that sweet girl doing something so awful."

"But she had access to the knives, and she said something really strange to me earlier. She said she'd been looking into buying a place, and said she had a partner with something in the works, and then she referenced changing things up a bit."

"Maybe she's trying to improve her life or something? Starting a business is a good thing, but it doesn't make her a killer."

"But the way she said it, it sounded like she was talking about Hamilton House."

"Every cook wants their own place. Even the two cooks are talking about getting out on their own, and they had access to the knives." She busied herself with papers on her desk. "'Sides, like I said before, Bobby wouldn't never sell the place."

"Can you get me in front of the cooks?"

She nodded. "One of them is in the kitchen here. He's helping me out until we can get the restaurant mess figured out. I'll call the other right quick."

"You do that, and I'll talk to suspect number one." I didn't think he was an actual suspect, but I felt all investigator like saying that.

I laid my cards on the table because there wasn't time to waste. The competition was the next day, and I had a to-do list five pages long. "Can you tell me what happened the morning Bobbie was killed?"

He removed the net from his curly brown hair and held it in his hand. "No, ma'am. You don't leave the kitchen in the morning. It's against the rules."

"I'm sorry?"

"Mr. Pruitt, he's got rules, and one of them is no cooks leave the kitchen in the morning until the prep work is complete."

"What if you have to use the restroom?"

"We got one back there."

"Oh. So you're sure no one left?"

"Yes, ma'am. Well, not the second assistant cooks, but

Maybelle, she did. She went to talk to Mr. Pruitt. Said she'd be back right quick."

"Did you see her leave?"

"Yes, ma'am. Said good luck as she walked out. She was goin' to talk to him about her decision to enter the competition. I knew he'd fire her, but she didn't care. Said she'd already had a plan anyway."

"Did she tell you her plan?"

"Yes, ma'am. She was wantin' to start her own restaurant. Said she wanted it done by the end of the year."

"Had she told Bobby?"

He shrugged. "I don't like getting in nobody's business if I don't have to. Gets me in all kinds of hot water when I do."

I could relate to that. "Did she happen to mention where she wanted to open her place?"

"No, ma'am, but she did say her partner was looking at a location, and she thought she'd get it."

"Did you notice Maybelle taking anything with her when she went to talk to Bobby?"

He pursed his lips and pushed them to the right side of his face, dragging his eyebrows together at the bridge of his nose. It wasn't a good look on him. "Can't say that I did."

"How did you get along with Bobby Pruitt?"

"I kept to my business and did as I was told. You do that with Mr. Pruitt and he treats you fine."

The other cook arrived and we had a very similar conversation.

"Well, that didn't help," Delphina said.

"It didn't hurt either. Even the cooks knew Maybelle had plans to open her own place. The first one even said she had a partner looking into it. I need to find out if anyone actually approached Bobby about buying the place. That may be the key to this whole thing."

"You know he left everything to me, right?"

"He did?"

She nodded. "Got himself some fancy attorney when his momma died, made sure his arrangements were made 'cause he said if something happened to him, he didn't want me having to handle that."

"And he left you his business? Do you know the attorney's name?"

"Sure do." She pulled a card out of her pocket. "Got to call him in a bit about a meetin' for next week."

"You should call him and find out if anyone's made any official offers or if Bobby ever brought them up. Maybelle's using his recipe in the competition, and she's looking to open her own place. That's awfully shady."

"If she killed Bobby, she won't get any of that. I'll make sure of it."

"So will the judge."

"Maybe she isn't as nice as she wants us to think."

"Desperate people do desperate things."

———

Olivia and I stayed up until two o'clock in the morning to get the competition to do list handled. We'd done all the prep work, and all that was left was the contestants' checks and making sure everything went as planned. After a few hours of sleep, I got up, showered, and went to get Austin ready for his dad to pick up, something I wasn't looking forward to, and didn't know about until Austin told me the night before.

When I tapped on his bedroom door he was awake, packed and ready to go. My heart hurt a little from that, but I was also relieved he'd begun to heal.

Scott came to the door and knocked. I couldn't recall him ever knocking on my parents' door, but it wasn't their door anymore. It was his ex-wife's. Austin sauntered over to let him in like he wasn't all that interested, but I knew better.

"Hey, Til, how's it going?"

I'd asked him to stop using his nickname for me, but he hadn't. I used to love it, but it no longer held the comfort and meaning it once did. "Good. And you?"

He shrugged.

"Oh, I hear congratulations are due. So, yeah, congratulations."

Austin coughed.

"Honey, go say goodbye to Cooper. He'll be lost without you." He hurried out, knowing a talk he didn't want to be a part of was coming.

I leaned against the kitchen counter, and Scott walked toward me. "I was going to tell you."

I stepped out of his path and crossed over to the other side of the kitchen. "I'm fine, really."

"Still, I should have said something."

"Listen, here's the thing. Austin is going out on a limb here, spending time with you. He wanted to stay for the barbecue competition this weekend. It's a big event here, and all his friends are going."

"Oh, I didn't know."

"No, you wouldn't have. Interesting timing though on your part. You're supposed to see him twice a month, and then when you don't, and suddenly decide you want to see him, what's he supposed to do, say no?"

He didn't have a reply.

"Just do me a favor, either be in or out of his life, but not both. He's a kid. He doesn't need that."

"I know."

"And he's really excited to be your best man, so treat him like you would someone in that position, someone like Steve—" I stopped myself. Steve was his best man in our wedding. Steve, the guy that stopped being friends with Scott after he found out about his affair. I liked Steve.

"Til—"

"Please don't call me that. It makes me ill."

"Okay, Ti—Chantilly, I'm sorry, okay? I'm intent on doing better, and I will. If you want, we'll stay in town this weekend so he can hang out with his friends at the competition. I can get a hotel."

I almost considered that, but the teeny part of bitterness still lingering, a bitterness I wasn't aware of until that moment, smacked me upside the head. "No, no, no. The last thing I need is to feel uncomfortable because you're here." I instantly hated myself for that. "Wait." I rubbed the back of my neck. "This isn't about me, and it's not my call. It's Austin's." I called our son back into the kitchen.

"Yeah?"

"Dad has an idea."

He was so excited, he actually showed emotion. "Yeah, for sure. We're staying."

"Great, then it's settled."

"You'd better check on hotels quick. This is a big thing, and I don't know if there's anything available."

"I'm on it." Scott smiled at me and then at Austin. "Let's get outta here, kiddo. Looks like your mom's got a lot on her plate, and we don't want to be in the way."

Austin waved, but I reached out, grabbed his shirt by the shoulder, and pulled him into a hug. "Let your momma kiss you, you big dork." I smothered the top of his head with kisses. It was all I could do not to squeeze him tight and keep him as close to me as possible and as far away from the person that broke our hearts.

But if my son could start to forgive his father, I needed to woman up and do it, too.

I pulled into the parking lot at the fields and into the first spot designated for competition staff. Many of the competitors were already there, and the field smelled like I was starving, even though I wasn't.

I found Olivia at the judges' quarters and set my things on a small table. She handed me a clipboard. "Hopefully you're rested because it's going to be a busy morning. You've got to inspect each of the contestants' booths and make sure everything is up to par with the rules." She flipped over the first page. "Here they are in case you need them. There aren't a lot, but there's a lot of competitors, so we can split the work. I'll take the back half and you hit the front? Sound good?"

I scanned the contestant map. "Sure, but I want these three in your section." I pointed to Rashid's, Julia and Jesse's and Maybelle's booths.

"Yes, ma'am."

I reviewed the rules, noting that each contestant could only have two coolers, two smokers, seven forks, and seven knives. "Who made these rules?"

"I don't know, but they've been this way as long as I can remember."

"Some of them are outdated, and others are ridiculous. We'll have to review these for next year. I see a lot of changes in this thing." I mumbled a few ideas out loud as I got busy.

Rashid had a small crowd of people in his booth, but to make sure everything was up to par, I needed them out. He understood, and out they went, except they all watched with curiosity and concern as I examined his ten by ten booth.

I went to open a cooler, but he stopped me. "No, no. You mustn't open that. It contains our special ingredient for the barbecue. Nobody can know."

"Rashid, I have to check everything. I'm sorry, but it's the rules of the competition. If I don't, and you've got something in here that doesn't meet the rules, you could be eliminated from the competition."

Panic took over his face. "But it is our secret recipe. We do not share that. What can I do?" He bounced on his toes. "I do not know how to handle this. I am very worried."

"Rashid," I spoke softly, hoping it would calm him. "I won't tell anyone your secret ingredient. I promise."

"No, no. This is what happens. This is why I was so angry at Mr. Pruitt. I just don't know."

"You told Bobby Pruitt your recipe?"

"No, no. I did not. He came into my restaurant when I was not there, and he saw, and he threatened to report me to the city council, he said that people would not want to eat my food. He promised to put me out of business."

My eyes widened. "Is there something dangerous in your recipe?"

"No, no. It is a family recipe. It is years old. Many years. We do not want it out to the public for it will be copied and no longer special."

"I promise you I will not share your recipe with a soul. You have my word."

He rushed over to an older woman and whispered in her ear. She nodded and then hugged him.

"I cannot reveal the recipe. It is sacred. We will be forever ruined."

I leaned against his large folding table. "This is why you went to talk to Bobby, isn't it? He found out your secret ingredient and threatened to tell, didn't he?"

He nodded over and over. "Yes, yes. I begged him to let it be. My grandmother, she is at unrest now because of it. I cannot lose now. I must win so her soul can be at peace."

I blew a hair away from my chin. "You didn't make amends, did you?"

Sweat pooled on his temples. "I did not murder Mr. Pruitt, Miss. Adair. I did not. I am not a violent man. When he threatened me again, I left. That is why I was there for only five minutes." He buried his face into his hands. "I should not have lied. It is not my personal nature. I am sorry."

"Things are tense right now, but it'll be okay. I promise you no one will know your secret recipe, but I do have to take a look inside that cooler or I'll have to disqualify you. Please help me here."

His eyes shifted between me and his small crowd of helpers. An older woman smiled and nodded once. He breathed a heavy sigh. "Yes, it is okay. I trust you."

"Thank you."

He opened the cooler and revealed his secret recipe ingredient.

Creamy peanut butter, at least twenty-five jars of the stuff.

I nodded, and he closed the lid quickly. I reviewed the rest of his space, noting that the knives he had near his smoker had brown blades with intricate carvings on them. I counted seven, and I picked one up and admired the carvings.

"My great-great grandfather made those. They're all I use to cook." He gently removed the knife from my hand. Rashid's fingers were long and thin, just like the rest of his body, but they were also damaged. I watched as he struggled to hold the knife steady. He forced his bent knuckles, riddled with large knots sticking out on both sides, to fold over the handle. His hand shook like my father's had.

"Rashid, do you have Parkinson's?"

He placed the knife on the small counter next to the smoker. "I am afraid so, but I am doing well."

"My father had it, too. I noticed your hands shaking."

He sighed. "It is hard. I am weaker now, but still able to work, and that is good. My son will take over for me when I cannot."

"But you want to find a larger location for your restaurant?"

He nodded. "Yes, yes. For my son. He is very strong, and has very large plans for the future. I would like to help him while I am still able."

"You're a good man, Rashid."

I believed him. There was no way a thin man with shaky hands could overcome Bobby Pruitt. Just no way.

I offered him my well wishes and good luck for the competition then headed to Maybelle's booth.

She gladly let me check her booth and chitchatted like nothing had happened, saying she was excited to move forward with her life.

Lonna Appleton came by and hugged her, completely disregarding me.

"Congratulations, Maybelle. I'm so excited for us," she said.

"Oh, I am just tickled pink. Things are finally falling into place, now that I'm out from Bobby Pruitt's wrath."

I glanced up from checking the two coolers behind her smoker. "Which recipe are you using?"

Lonna stuck her nose where it didn't belong. "What does that matter?"

"Because the rules say the recipe can't be one of a former contestant, and Maybelle mentioned she wanted to use Bobby's."

"Well, I don't see why she can't now that he's dead. I'm sure he'd appreciate it. It would be like she was honoring him."

Maybe Lonna had a friend after all? I rolled my eyes. "Lonna, we have rules, and they don't really concern you."

"Well, of course they do. This is my business partner right here."

I blinked. "You're kidding, right?"

"Oh, she mustn't have said anything yet, but we're going into business together. Opening a restaurant, and we've got the perfect location in mind."

Maybelle beamed with excitement. "We sure do, partner. Lonna has been pressing me to move on with my life and start my own business for some time. She finally convinced me, with the help of Bobby firing me, of course."

A location? Was she talking about Hamilton House? She couldn't have leased it, not yet. Delphina would have known. "That's great. But I'm afraid you still can't use his recipe."

"Oh, I'm not. I gave up that thought immediately after I said it. I want to build my reputation as the best barbecue in town, not copy his."

"And things are finally falling into place," Lonna said. "Because of my hard work."

Maybelle nodded and hugged Lonna's waist, squeezing her face into Lonna's arm. "She's the best."

I smiled and got back to business as the two of them whispered about their new adventure. Sitting in a plastic shopping bag on the ground near the smoker was a set of knives. Ones exactly like the one Delphina showed me. "How many of those do you have? You're only allowed seven."

She stepped over and emptied the bag. "One, two, three—" she moved each one as she said a number. "four, five, six, seven. Didn't break the rule."

No, but the knives looked just like I'd expected, even with the slightly curved and sharper blade.

Rashid was off my list, but Maybelle was still tops on it.

Jesse wasn't at the Lye's booth, but Julia was again getting everything set up. The smoker was up and running, and from the smell of it, something yummy was smoking inside it.

Of all the smells, I had to admit theirs was the best. I didn't know what they did with the meat, but whatever it was, it made my mouth water.

"I'm here to check on your booth, just make sure everything's up to par."

"You won't find any problems," she said. She stepped outside of the booth. "Go ahead."

"I'm surprised Jesse isn't here. We'll be open to the public in a few hours." I checked the coolers and under their work table.

"He just needed to run and pick up something."

"I hope it doesn't interfere with the competition for your sake." I wished I could take that back immediately after I'd said it.

"Nothing is going to interfere with the competition, Ms. Adair."

"I didn't mean it like that."

"I don't care how you meant it, but if you continue to treat us with suspicion, I'm going to ask they remove you from the judge list."

I stopped, turned around, and looked at her. "Do what you must."

I made sure to check every possible area for knives that matched or were similar to the one Del showed me. I counted six, not seven on the work table. "You know you can have one more knife, right?" I counted her forks also. "And two more forks."

"Jesse left his favorite knife at home. That's where he went."

I signed off on her paperwork and rushed out of her booth. I called Olivia on the way to my car.

"Hey Miss Chantilly, what's up?"

"Olivia, I had to run out, but I'll be back, okay?"

"Um, I...I guess. What about the booth checks?"

"I'm going to need you to finish up my side. I'm sorry. Maybe one of the other judges can help?"

"I'll take care of it. Is everything all right?"

"Yes, it's fine. I'll be back soon."

I headed straight to Jesse Lye's house, but made one more call on my way.

Del called as I stepped out of my car in the Lye's driveway. I clicked decline and walked at a fast clip to his front door.

"Be right there," he hollered from inside. When he opened the door, his anticipating smile dropped into an annoyed grimace. "I'm heading there now. Julia called me. I had a feeling you'd show up here."

That just led me to believe he was guilty, but I already thought that anyway. "Why would you think I was coming here?"

"You counted the knives and one is missing. Bobby Pruitt was stabbed. Everyone knows that now. What do you think we think?"

"Did you do it?"

A car pulled up behind me. We both looked at it and said in unison, "I called the police."

"Wait, what?" I asked.

"I don't want you harassing me anymore."

Jack walked up and shook his head. "Chantilly." He nodded to Jesse. "Mr. Lye."

"I want her arrested for harassment. This is ridiculous."

"Mr. Lye, can I have a few minutes with Ms. Adair alone, please?"

Jesse checked his watch. "Fine, but make it quick. I got to get back to the competition." He stepped back into his house and sat on the couch.

Jack's nose flared. "What do you think you're doing?"

"The knife, Jack. He came back for his favorite knife. Don't you think that's a little odd? And they all look just like the ones at Hamilton House."

He leaned his head back and mumbled something that included dear God, but I couldn't catch the rest. "Chantilly, stop. You do your job, and I'll do mine."

"But I'm a suspect in a murder, and I'm innocent. I need to find who did it. If I don't, Austin will live with Scott and his soon to be wife, and I'll spend the rest of my life in prison for a crime I didn't commit, and Lord knows how many people have died in those places, and I can't tell you how creepy that would be, seeing their ghosts. Agnes Hamilton is scary enough, believe me, and I just—"

He stopped my incessant babbling. "I don't even want to know what you're talking about, but stop. Just stop. We're closing in on the killer, and you're going to mess it up if you keep doing this stuff. Now get out of here. I'll try to calm Mr. Lye down, but you may end up in jail on harassment charges. I'll do my best."

"But who do—"

He pointed toward my car. "Chantilly, go. Now."

I sulked away like a child scolded in class.

As I backed out, I watched Jesse's arms flail with energy and determination. I worried I'd be calling Scott to bail me out of jail in a few minutes, and prayed Jack could calm the man quickly.

CHAPTER 12

J called Olivia to let her know I was on my way back. I didn't mention my stern talking to by Jack, nor did I bring up the fact that the police were getting close to solving the case. I was just happy that Jack had convinced Jesse Lye to not press charges against me since I'd promised to stay away from them.

I drove to the park with my tail between my legs—filled with embarrassment and wishing I'd handled things differently.

Hindsight was twenty-twenty for sure.

"Oh, can you stop by the office right quick? I need at least two pads of paper. I'm going through it like crazy."

"Sure, no problem. Anything else?"

"Oh, Miss Delphina called me. She wants you to call her right away."

I dialed Del's line and she picked up immediately. "Spoke to the attorney."

"And?"

"Lonna Appleton extended an offer to purchase Bobby's restaurant two months ago, and as the attorney said, Bobby laughed in her face. Just yesterday she requested to re-submit the offer, and that she would be interested in leasing the space if it wasn't for sale."

"Oh my gosh."

"That ain't no coincidence."

"I need to go." I disconnected the call and called Jack again immediately. "You're one lucky girl, you know that?"

I ignored him. "It's Lonna, Jack. I think Lonna killed Bobby."

"What? What're you talking about?"

"Did you know she's partnering with Maybelle to open a restaurant?"

"Where'd you hear that?"

"From them. And she made an offer to buy Bobby's place two months ago, but he turned her down."

"Are you sure?"

"He left everything to Delphina. She just told me the attorney told her Lonna submitted the offer again and offered to lease the property if she couldn't buy it."

He was silent for a moment, and then asked when I'd be back at the park.

"In a bit. I have to stop and pick something up at the museum first."

"Call me as soon as you get there. I don't want you saying a thing to anyone, okay?"

"Yes, sir."

I pulled up to the historical society and threw my car in park. I jogged to the entrance, unlocked the door and slammed it behind me. In a hurry, I searched Olivia's office first, not thinking to just go to the room where we stored everything.

The door to the storage room shut behind me. I grabbed the broken Tiffany lamp and flipped around, ready to beat whomever was behind me. Standing next to the door was Agnes Hamilton, her white wedding dress dancing on the ground, a noose dangling from her neck.

I flinched and stepped back, falling into the table behind me.

"I uh…" I didn't know what to say. My hands shook, and I dropped the lamp onto the ground.

She looked down at the lamp base. "You just keep that for protection." The lamp floated up to my hand, and I latched onto it. "Now, hurry, leave."

I stared at her, confused. "What? No, I don't…please. I don't." I didn't know what I was trying to say. Words flew out of my mouth, but made no sense, and my mind ran a marathon of circles inside my head. "I…"

A scene flashed before me, and I was again standing there, frozen in time, in the past, watching something horrific happen before me.

Bobby Pruitt sat at his desk as someone in black entered.

"What're you doing here?"

The person walked over to Bobby and stood behind him, leaned forward and kissed his cheek. He smiled and laughed, and then his mouth fell open and he choked out his last words, "What the…Lonna baby, what'd you do?"

My eyes popped open. "Oh no."

The spirit moved closer and whispered, "Hurry. She's coming." A moment later, she disappeared through the door.

I ran to it, flung it open, but she was gone. I heard the main door close downstairs. "Olivia? Is that you?" I rushed down the stairs, and all dressed in black, just like I'd seen moments before in my mind, was Lonna Appleton. I stopped short on the stairs. "Oh, Lonna. I thought you were Olivia." I froze in place, not sure what to do. I couldn't make a run for it, not with her right there, but going upstairs was a big mistake, too. I decided to play the caring card because it was all I could come up with in the moment. "Is everything okay?" I tightened my grip on the lamp base.

"You know the answer to that, don't you? Why do you always have to win? Why can't you just let me have the glory for a change? I was doing great until you came back to town and screwed things up. This is all your fault." She moved a step closer to the stairs, and that's when I noticed the knife in her hand. The knife with a similar handle to practically every knife I'd seen lately.

"Lonna, you don't want to do this. Really, let's talk about this, please."

"Oh bless your heart, you think I care about what you have to say? Honey, you are so wrong. I've never cared about you or anything you've had to say, and it's time I show you that."

"Why'd you kill him? Because he wouldn't sell the place? Did you think if you charmed him by being his girlfriend, he'd sell it to you?"

She stepped up the first stair, only five away from me, and paused. "You...you don't know anything."

"I know you tried to buy his restaurant, and he wouldn't sell, and you must have come onto him to try and change his mind, but when that didn't work, you killed him."

"I could make that place much better than him, and he knew it. He just wouldn't budge, no matter what I did. I had to do it. When he figured out what was going on, he threatened to tell Jack, and I couldn't let that happen." She laughed. "I just walked right in through the cellar and tiptoed upstairs without even a glance from those stupid cooks. Even Maybelle." She laughed. "They all were so scared of Bobby, but not me. I knew exactly what he wanted, and I gave it to him."

Yuck. I hoped that wouldn't be the last thing stuck in my mind when she killed me. I couldn't bare living with that thought for an eternity. "You were there when Rashid came, weren't you?"

She laughed. "His stupid secret ingredient." She waved the knife as she spoke. "Peanut butter. Bobby threw him out, and he threw Maybelle out, too."

I backed up a step. I had no choice. She was too close. "You're using her, aren't you? You don't care about her. The only person you care about is yourself." I thought about Jack and how she acted so enamored with him. "You don't even care about Jack, do you?"

"I do, and he cared about me until you messed that all up. But it doesn't matter. You'll be dead and buried, and who do you think will be there to comfort him?"

"Jack said he was closing in on a suspect. He must know it's you."

She climbed up another step and laughed. "He doesn't know a thing, and he won't, because you won't be around to tell him." She charged up the last four stairs to me, wielding the knife out in front of her like a crazy woman.

I screamed and shifted to my right, hoping to dodge her, but instead I tripped again, on the same darn stair I'd tripped on the first time. As Lonna came at me, I forced the weight of my fall into her and pushed with all my might. If I was going down those stairs again, I was bringing Lonna Appleton with me.

I wrapped my arms around her as we tumbled down the last few steps and onto the marble landing.

The thud of her skull smacking the marble tile sent acid shooting up my esophagus.

She didn't move.

I lay there on top of her breathing heavily for a moment, not sure what to do. But Lonna wasn't moving. I pushed myself off and up onto my forearms and that's when I saw the blood. Lonna's eyes were closed.

I didn't dare touch her neck, but I needed to see if she was breathing. I leaned my head gently onto her chest and felt it rise and lower below me.

My phone. I needed my phone. I didn't have it on me. I must have left it in my car. I climbed off the ground and as I stood, I saw Lonna's phone a few feet away. Jack's number popped up on the caller ID.

"It's Chantilly. Get an ambulance to the historical society. It's Lonna. She's hurt."

———

Jack walked out through the emergency room doors and into the waiting area. Del had met me there, after I begged Jack to let me come to the hospital, too. Even though I didn't like Lonna, and I knew she was a killer, I didn't want to be responsible for her death. She was a mother, too. Her children needed her whether that meant they visited her in prison or a mental institution.

He made eye contact with the officer in the room and nodded toward the exit. When the officer left, he sat next to me. "She's going to be okay."

"I didn't push her if that's what she's telling you."

Del defended my honor. "No way would this sweet woman push anyone like that."

He smiled. "She confessed. She told me everything. She thought you already had."

I covered my mouth with my hand. "Oh, I'm so sorry. For what she did to Bobby, and for what she did to you."

Jack nodded. "Didn't I say dating was a problem for me?"

"Something like that."

He sat silent for a moment. "You should get back to the park. The competition needs you."

"We got it handled," Del said.

"I'm glad, because there's something I need to take care of right away."

"Can I help?" she asked. "Nope, I have to do this myself, and you need to get to the competition to help Olivia."

I called Olivia to let her know I was okay. After ten minutes of her expressing her joy, I had to cut her off. "Olivia, I've got to take care of something, but I'll be back in a bit. Del's on her way, okay?"

I walked into the office and right under the yellow crime scene tape on the stairs. I gathered everything I had about Josiah and stuffed it all into a file folder. I pulled up the Hamilton House document I'd written before and added information about Bobby, giving him the respect he deserved, and I felt, honored Hamilton House. I printed it out and rushed over to the mayor's office, hoping I'd catch him before he left for the competition.

"Is the mayor in?"

"Yes, I'll grab him." She stepped away.

I tapped my foot while I waited. I had no idea what I was going to say, but I had enough to at least argue my changes.

"Ms. Adair, I heard what happened. You've had a busy day. Are you okay? I'm leaving in a few minutes to give the official speech at the competition. Do you think you'll be able to continue?"

"Yes, Mr. Mayor, but something's come up, and I need you to sign off on it."

He swung his arm toward his office. "After you then."

I handed him the file. "I'm submitting a change to the Hamilton House's historical summary. It includes a memorial of sorts to Bobby Pruitt, but there are a few other changes you need to see. Olivia Castleberry has done some research, and we believe strongly that Agnes Hamilton didn't kill herself. I think it's important to note that, for Agnes."

He flipped through the papers and smiled. "Has Agnes requested this?" There was a fun tone to his voice.

"In a matter of speaking, yes."

He glanced over the top of his glasses at me. "Interesting." He read the emails about Josiah Dilts. "Mr. Dilts had quite the reputation, didn't he? Seemed to be on shaky ground here. I remember as a child hearing these kinds of rumors." He closed the file. "I don't see a problem with this, but we'll need the City Council's approval."

"I'd appreciate your help with that. This is important to me."

He looked me in the eye. "You almost died today, and you saved Castleberry from a murderer. I think I can make it happen."

———

The event ended at nine o'clock, and after we prepared for the final day and closed up, Delphina handed me a key. "Go, give the closure. She needs it. Bobby needs it, too."

"Would you like to come?"

"No way." She fell into a lawn chair and rubbed her left leg. "I'm all sorts of give out, and my feet are killing me. I need a vacation from this thing or I won't make it out alive."

I raised my eyebrows.

"Bad choice of words?"

"Yes, ma'am."

I wrapped my hand around the key. "Thank you. I'll see you in the morning."

"No, you'll call me when it's done. I need to know you're okay."

"I will."

I drove over to Hamilton House and unlocked the back door into the kitchen. The entire place was black, and my teeth chattered. I was scared, but I wasn't sure why, or of what. It wasn't like the spirits there wanted to hurt me. At least not the one I'd already seen. I'd just started a new phase of my life, and adding spirit seer to it scared me, plain and simple.

A dim light glowed in the dining hall. I walked toward it, each step slow and hesitant.

There in the room, her bridal gown flowing beneath her, the noose dangling from her neck, stood Agnes Hamilton.

"I've told them the truth. It'll be okay now."

She smiled, and the noose disappeared. "He thanks you, too." She rotated to the left, and behind her floated a cloudy, almost transparent Bobby Joe Pruitt. He smiled at me, and they both disappeared.

"Holy wow." I stood there for a moment, shocked, amazed, and flabbergasted.

When Jack tapped me on the back, I jumped and screamed. "Oh my gosh. You scared me."

He pointed to the places where Agnes and Bobby had just been. "Performing another séance?"

I shrugged. "In a matter of speaking, yes."

He shook his head. "Let's get out of here. I could use a drink. Got any beer?"

"Sweet tea work for ya? There's a lot of that at the competition."

"Sure thing."

I glanced back behind me one more time as we left the dining room, but we were definitely alone.

"Can you give me a minute? I need to make a quick call."

"Sure. I'll be outside."

I removed my phone from my pocket and dialed Angela Panther.

"You did good."

"How do you know?"

"I have my ways," she said.

"I'm not sure I want to know them."

"It'll be okay now. They're both where they belong."

"Are you sure?"

"Not one hundred percent, but pretty close. You never know with the dead. They can surprise us."

"Hopefully I won't have to worry about it again."

She laughed. "Yeah, I thought that once too, but Chantilly, there will be others."

"How do you know?"

"Your dad told me, and he told you too, remember?"

The End

GHOSTS ARE PEOPLE TOO:
Chantilly Adair Paranormal Cozy Mystery #2

When her best friend Gen comes from Birmingham for an extended visit, psychic medium Chantilly Adair can't wait to show her Castleberry, Georgia. Excited to introduce her to what makes her home town so unique, Chantilly plans to throw a party the size of Atlanta's Mercedes Stadium. Though she hasn't attempted an event that big since her own wedding, she's ready and willing to take the ball and run with it.

But when trouble comes to town in the form of her best friend's soon-to-be ex-husband, threatening both Chantilly and Gen, and winds up dead in the cellar of a local historical property, her plans change.

The cops can't find a suspect, other than Gen, of course.

Now, for Chantilly to clear her best friend, she'll need help from the property's owner, who just happens to be dead...

Get your copy today at
CarolynRidderAspenson.com

YOU MIGHT ALSO ENJOY...

The Lily Sprayberry Realtor Cozy Mystery Series

Deal Gone Dead

Decluttered and Dead

Signed, Sealed and Dead

Bidding War Break-In

Open House Heist

Realtor Rub Out

Foreclosure Fatality

Lily Sprayberry Novellas

The Scarecrow Snuff Out

The Claus Killing

Santa's Little Thief

The Chantilly Adair Paranormal Cozy Mystery Series

Get Up and Ghost

Ghosts Are People Too

Praying For Peace

Ghost From the Grave

Haunting Hooligans: A Chantilly Adair Novella

The Pooch Party Cozy Mystery Series

Pooches, Pumpkins, and Poison

Hounds, Harvest, and Homicide

Dogs, Dinners, and Death

The Holiday Hills Witch Cozy Mystery Series

There's a New Witch in Town

Witch This Way

The Angela Panther Mystery Series

Unfinished Business

Unbreakable Bonds

Uncharted Territory

Unexpected Outcomes

Unbinding Love

The Christmas Elf

The Ghosts

Undetermined Events

The Event

The Favor

Other Books

Mourning Crisis (The Funeral Fakers Series)

Join Carolyn's Newsletter List at

CarolynRidderAspenson.com

You'll receive a free novella as a thank you!

ACKNOWLEDGMENTS

Thank you to my wonderful editor Jen, and my favorite proof-reader JC Wing, and my friends and family who've supported me as I've traveled along this writing journey.

ABOUT CAROLYN

Carolyn Ridder Aspenson writes sassy, southern cozy mysteries featuring imperfect women with a flair for telling it like it is. Her stories focus on relationships, whether they're between friends, family members, couples, townspeople, or strangers, because ultimately, it's relationships that make a story.

Now an empty-nester, Carolyn lives in the Atlanta suburbs with her husband, two Pit Bull-Boxer mix dogs and two cantankerous cats, but you'll often find her at a local coffee shop people-watching (and listening.) Or as she likes to call it: plotting her next novel.

Join Carolyn's mailing list at
CarolynRidderAspenson.com

CPSIA information can be obtained
at www.ICGtesting.com
Printed in the USA
LVHW111442200720
661135LV00003B/685

9 781951 249939